Lily met his gaze, and a silent question floated between them.

Wes wasn't going to say that he already knew the real reason she'd gone to the prison that day. She wasn't ready for that. But he could see how the prospect of the entire town knowing bothered her.

Wandering to the window behind her desk, she looked through it and didn't say anything.

He waited a few beats, but when she didn't move, he went to stand behind her. She looked up and over her shoulder at him when he touched her arm.

"If I could stop the gossip, I would," he said, and he meant it.

When she turned to face him, he saw how his declaration had eased some of her tension. Moving closer, she touched his face with her hand. "I believe you."

★★★

Dear Reader,

It was a true privilege to work with so many talented and friendly authors on THE COLTONS OF MONTANA. This was my first continuity. Not only was it fun, it was also a challenge. The corroborative effort was rewarding and showed me a new side to writing. I love to be pushed like that. Growth is an essential ingredient for me as a writer, because I am a firm believer that you should never stop learning and trying new things.

The Librarian's Secret Scandal is special to me because it involves a wounded heroine who refuses to crumble. Bad things happen to us and still we have to move forward. Sometimes that isn't easy. It's hard to stay afloat on a raft of positive energy when that energy seems to have all but dried up. It takes strength to throw that negativity overboard and adjust your course, set your sights on happier times and never let the bad ones drag you under. Sure, there may be some rough spots along the way, but you'll arrive at the end of your trip stronger than ever.

Lily Masterson faces adversity and never gives up. What a worthy addition to THE COLTONS OF MONTANA. I hope you'll feel the same.

Jennie

JENNIFER MOREY

The Librarian's Secret Scandal

ROMANTIC

SUSPENSE

With special thanks to Jennifer Morey for her contribution to THE COLTONS OF MONTANA.

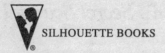

SILHOUETTE BOOKS

Recycling programs for this product may not exist in your area.

ISBN-13: 978-0-373-27694-3

THE LIBRARIAN'S SECRET SCANDAL

Books by Jennifer Morey

Silhouette Romantic Suspense

★*The Secret Soldier* #1526
★*Heiress Under Fire* #1578
Blackout at Christmas #1583
    "Kiss Me on Christmas"
★*Unmasking the Mercenary* #1606
The Librarian's Secret Scandal #1624

★All McQueen's Men

JENNIFER MOREY

Two-time 2009 RITA® Award nominee and Golden Quill winner for Best First Book for *The Secret Soldier,* Jennifer Morey writes contemporary romance and romantic suspense. Project manager du jour, she works for the space systems segment of a satellite imagery and information company and lives in sunny Denver, Colorado. She can be reached through her Web site, www.jennifermorey.com, on Facebook and at jmorey2009@gmail.com.

To my homey. There is no other hero for me.

Patience and Keyren for inviting me to participate in this romping continuity. Susan, for her never-ending brainstorming energy. My twin sister, Jackie, and the rest of my family for all their support.

And as always, Mom, who got me going down this path.

Chapter 1

The smell of stale air and cleaning chemicals lingered as Lily Masterson left Montana State Prison. Sunlight made her blink a few times, bringing her out of a fog of hugely unsettling emotions. She couldn't even begin to categorize them. Her nerves were a jumbled tangle of friction. Her stomach still churned. Her heart still beat heavily. A sob lodged in her throat. She hated that.

"Maybe you should wait a few minutes before you drive back to Honey Creek," the victims' officer said.

Lily didn't know what a typical prison worker was supposed to look like, but this one resembled more of a schoolmarm with her short, curly brown hair, round glasses and short, plump frame. The woman had met her at the prison entrance when she'd first arrived and stayed close through the parole hearing.

"I'm fine." It was a lie, but all she wanted was to get away from this place.

"Are you sure? Most victims don't come to these hearings alone. We usually meet them somewhere in town and drive them here."

Well, Lily wasn't like most people, then. She refused to succumb to that kind of weakness. It made her helpless, and she wasn't.

"Yes, I'm sure. Thanks for asking."

The truth was she'd barely made it through the hearing. While one part of her struggled with the reminder of the trauma she'd suffered, the other was mad as hell. She'd thought she was over this by now. Facing Brandon Gates shouldn't have been as hard as it had been. That's the part that made her mad. Why was she crumbling after she'd worked so hard to be strong? She'd gone through extensive therapy and aggressive self-defense classes. She'd picked herself up and started a new life and damn it, no one was going to take that away from her. Not again.

But being that close to Brandon Gates for the first time in fifteen years had thrown her. Crushed her. Talking about how he'd violated her and its devastating effect on her while he stared across the room like a dead deer was even worse. He hadn't looked at her, but his demeanor, his presence, still bothered her.

The victims' officer kept pace beside her. Lily thought she'd walk her to the exit and then let her be on her way, but apparently the woman was going to escort her all the way to her truck. Lily didn't want that. She'd talked to the woman before the hearing and they'd had a nice conversation, but it was time to leave.

"I can make it from here," she told the woman with a forced smile.

"Sometimes seeing them after so long is more disturbing than you think, and that's okay. It's perfectly natural to feel that way."

Lily was sure the officer had seen a lot of women break down after testifying at their rapist's parole hearing, but she didn't want to be one of them. "I'm fine, thanks."

Lily walked with the officer a few more steps and then stopped. The officer stopped, too, and seemed to understand Lily's growing impatience.

She handed her a business card. "All right, but if you need to talk to anyone, just give me a call. I can help you find someone good."

Lily took the card even though she had no intention of using this. She'd already gone through therapy. She refused to depend on that again. She'd moved on. This was just a minor setback. Chances were he wouldn't be released anyway. What board would do that after hearing her testimony?

"You'll be notified of the board's decision in about a week. Maybe less."

Lily nodded with another forced smile and started walking again. "You take care now," the woman called after her.

Lily kept walking, glancing back once to make sure she was finally rid of the woman. Seeing the officer heading back toward the prison settled her nerves a notch.

Reaching her Dodge Ram pickup truck, she kicked the front tire on her way to the driver's door to vent some of her frustration. It wasn't supposed to be like this. She was supposed to go to the parole hearing and hold her head high, show that dirty rat how strong she was. Climbing into the truck, she sat there for a minute, unable to shake her tension. She couldn't let her daughter see her like this. Not on top of all the talk flying around Honey Creek. She'd expected some talk around town, but she hadn't expected it to be as bad as it was. That was *two* things she'd underestimated.

Starting the engine, she wiped an escaped tear and backed out of the parking space. She drove toward the end of the row a little faster than she should have. Okay, a lot faster. She couldn't wait to get away, to put the prison behind her and out of sight. The residual image of Brandon's face lurked in her mind, the way he stayed focused on the parole board and ignored her. Would it have been better if he had acknowledged her?

Her stomach churned with nausea. Maybe once she returned to Honey Creek she'd recover.

A black SUV crossed in front of her. She didn't see it coming and didn't have time to avoid a collision. She slammed on her brakes, but her truck hit the SUV broadside. Her airbag exploded and her mind blanked for a second.

When she could think again, she saw that she'd sent the SUV head-on into a light pole. Its front end was crushed. So was the passenger side. Her truck didn't appear to have sustained much damage and the engine was still running. Her heart hammered and the shock of the wreck intensified the tremble in her limbs.

A man stepped out of the driver's side of the SUV. He was tall and muscular but lean. Lily opened her truck door and hopped out, steadying her wobbly legs as she approached the man.

"I am so sorry. Are you all right?" she said.

Rubbing the back of his neck, he stopped when she did, his eyes full of annoyance.

When he didn't answer, she asked, "D-do you want me to…call for help?" She'd left her cell phone in the truck. She started to turn.

"No. Don't do that. I'm okay."

She faced him again. He'd lowered his hand and now his gaze took her in, a slow and observant once-over.

She stiffened a little. At least he wasn't as annoyed anymore. "Your neck…"

"It'll be sore for a few days but I'm all right."

After studying her face a bit longer, he glanced back at

his SUV and then walked to the front. There, he stood and surveyed the damage.

Lily was mortified. She wanted to crawl out of her skin and escape until this was over.

"I have insurance," she said quickly.

He looked at her.

"I—I was…I guess I was…a little distracted," she stammered.

"Places like this have that effect," he said.

Was he kidding? She didn't know what to say.

"It's probably going to be totaled," he said.

Great. She couldn't remember what her deductable was. A thousand probably. And her rates would go up after this, too.

"That's all right." As if.

"I liked my SUV," he said.

She hadn't thought of it like that. "I'm sorry." Could she disappear now?

The victims' officer came running toward them. She must have barely made it into the building when she'd noticed the crash.

Here we go, Lily thought. Lord, she wanted to go home.

"Oh, my God…are you two okay?" The officer stopped, breathing rapidly from exertion.

"Yes, we're fine," Lily said. "Neither one of us is hurt, but I'll call the police for an accident report and we'll be on our way." She tapped the toe of her shoe on the pavement and looked toward the road leading to the checkpoint.

The officer followed her look and then her gaze passed over the wreckage of the man's truck. "One of you isn't going anywhere without help. You'll need a tow."

"We probably need an accident report," Lily repeated, knowing she sounded harried. "You know…for insurance. So as soon as we call.…" She could drive home.

"We don't need to call anyone to come out here," the man said.

She stopped tapping her foot. "Really?"

"No one was hurt, and this is a private parking lot. All we need to do is stop by the sheriff's office and fill out a form for insurance."

"Oh. Okay. Good." Then all they needed was a tow truck. How long would that take?

His eyes grew more curious and then he really looked at her. It made her nervous. As if she wasn't nervous enough.

"Maybe I should get someone to drive you home," the officer said to her. "You look a little shaken."

"No. I can drive."

"You were just in an accident."

This lady was really starting to irritate her. Did she hound all the victims who came here? Lily didn't respond, just looked toward the road again. Oh, to be on it, driving away from here, on her way home.

"Wait a minute," the man said, which brought her head back around. "You look familiar."

How could he possibly know her?

"Where are you from?" he asked.

She didn't want to tell him.

"Wes Colton." He stuck out his hand. "Honey Creek County sheriff."

Momentarily stunned, she numbly took his hand. Colton. He was a Colton?

"You're from Honey Creek?" she asked, her astonishment coming out in her tone.

He smiled. "Yeah. You're Lily Masterson, right? You took over for Mary Walsh at the library."

"That's me," Lily said, cringing inside. The resident bad girl. There was only one reason he recognized her. All the gossip. Honey Creek was rampant with it these days.

"You know each other?" the officer cut in.

"No," Lily all but snapped.

"Not really," Wes answered conversationally. "We both live in Honey Creek. It's not far from here."

"I know where that town is." The officer smiled. "Quite a coincidence, wouldn't you say?"

Quite.

He nodded toward the prison. "Might be a bad sign that we're both here."

Lily was getting good at forcing humor. She laughed.

Great. Would he guess why she was here? If the victims' officer didn't give her away....

She glanced at the woman. Her eyes had widened but she remained quiet.

"What brings you here?" she asked Wes.

"I came here to see my brother."

Of course. She remembered. Damien Colton was in prison for murder, except the man he had supposedly murdered had recently turned up—dead again. Damien was Wes Colton's brother. Talk about his impending release was all over town. Lily looked more closely at him. He was handsome and young. She thought she remembered someone saying he was thirty-three, which was too young for her forty years.

"What about you?" he asked, and she wished she would have kept her mouth shut.

"Oh...." How was she going to answer that? No one from Honey Creek knew what had happened to her. "I was just... visiting a friend."

The officer angled her head a little, a silent question in her eyes.

Lily ignored her, but she couldn't ignore Wes. The amusement that had pulled a smile from his mouth faded.

Surely he'd heard all the rumors. Some weren't rumors, either. Before she'd left Honey Creek, she'd done anything and everything to spite her holier-than-thou parents. That was so long ago, though, and so much had changed since then. She'd changed. Why was it so hard for everyone to see that?

"What kind of trouble did your friend get into to land himself here?" he asked.

She thought fast. "Robbery."

The officer's eyebrows lifted.

"Must be someone close to you if you're willing to visit him here."

"He's just a…a…friend."

The officer's eyebrows lowered and her eyes turned sympathetic. She knew why Lily was lying.

Lily met her gaze and hoped she read the message not to say anything. When the officer remained a silent observer, she didn't know if that was worse. Pity was for the vulnerable.

"You've been away from Honey Creek for a while," Wes said, appearing oblivious to the exchange. "What brought you back?"

Another subject she didn't particularly want to discuss. But he wasn't pressing on her reason for being here so she wouldn't complain. "My dad. His health isn't so great right now. Stage two stomach cancer. He's gone through the surgery, but he's still in treatment and we don't know how things will progress from here. I came back to help him. Without Mom around it's hard for him to care for himself."

He nodded and his blue eyes showed his admiration. They also showed self-assurance and intelligence that went along with his honorable reputation. She checked his left hand. No ring.

"That's very kind of you to do that," the officer said, sounding out of place in the conversation. Was that because she'd noticed Lily looking at Wes?

Checking for a ring. Oh, lord….

He had really nice hands. She'd heard he was a nice man, too. And a sheriff….

Something about that appealed to her.

She stopped herself short. Why was she thinking like this? She hadn't been back in Honey Creek long, and was too caught up in the gossip going around about her to pay much attention to potential love interests. She didn't want to get involved with anyone. So why had those thoughts even crossed her mind? Was she interested in Wes? He was attractive, but…

Lily tipped her head back and looked up at the big, blue sky. "At least the weather is nice."

Wes looked up with her, but not for very long. He was studying her again.

"Sure is," the officer said, drawing out the word *sure* suggestively.

And Lily snapped her head down to see the officer smiling.

The officer turned to Wes. "So, you're a sheriff?"

"Yes. Honey Creek County."

"Oh, well," the officer beamed, "Lily's in good hands then."

Wes chuckled.

Lily loved the sound. "Should we call for a tow now?"

"Of course," the officer cooed. "And then maybe you could let Sheriff Colton drive you back home in your truck, Lily," the officer suggested, doing a bad job of pretending to be nonchalant. "He'll be needing a rental car anyway." Her smile was more genuine now, but held a tinge of slyness. Maybe she understood why Lily had lied and only wanted to make sure she made it home all right.

Not.

The officer had noticed their exchange and was now match-making. Was she like this with all the victims?

"Sure." Anything to be gone from here as soon as humanly

possible. She looked at Wes. "I can drive you back to Honey Creek."

He dipped his head. "I'd appreciate that."

After the tow truck had left with Wes's SUV and the prison worker had gone back into the building, Wes got into Lily's pickup. As she started the engine, he covertly looked at her. She had thick, long black hair and a pair of amazing blue eyes. Her breasts were just the right size and shape in the short-sleeved collared cotton shirt she wore, and she looked nice in the knee-length jean skirt.

She started driving. He hadn't argued over who should drive. He thought he should, but he also had the impression she needed the control…or the sense of it. He faced forward. The truck was quiet and she stayed focused on the road.

It was strange thinking of her as the wild and uninhibited woman she'd been before she left town. She seemed like such a lady now. Professional. Friendly, if a little nervous. He wasn't sure if it was the accident or the real reason she'd come to the prison. He knew she hadn't been telling him the truth when she said she'd come to see someone. She got a scared look when she'd told him. And the way she'd said *just a friend* signaled a lie. *Just a friend,* yeah, right. Whoever she'd come to see, he wasn't her friend. Besides, that whole exchange with the prison officer had been weird.

He'd gotten good at recognizing when someone wasn't on the up-and-up. Too many times he'd trusted his first impressions only to learn it was all a facade, especially with women.

Now he was more than a little curious about what had brought Lily to the prison. He'd make a call in the morning. He knew people at the prison.

"Have you always lived in Honey Creek?" Lily asked.

Good. She felt like talking. "No, I moved away after high

school and joined the navy." He didn't want to get into his SEAL training. It had been a youthful impulse, but as soon as he'd grown up enough he'd realized the daredevil employment wasn't really all that impressive. It didn't pay well, either. Neither did being a sheriff in a little town like Honey Creek, but he liked the sense of community and being close to his family—however dramatic they could be at times.

"How did you go from the service to law enforcement?" she asked.

"After I was with the navy, I went through training and worked as a peace officer for a while. Worked my way up the ranks and then ran for sheriff here."

"You've been back some time then?"

"A few years."

She nodded conversationally.

He was glad she didn't ask more about his background with the navy. "You have a daughter, don't you?" he asked just in case, redirecting the topic.

The smile that formed on her profile was warm and lovely. The sight revved his interest. When he'd first seen her get out of her truck, he'd almost forgotten all about the wreck. She was tall, which he liked since he was six-two, and slender and she had smooth skin.

"Yes," she answered. "May. She's fourteen going on thirty. Or so she thinks."

Wes smiled in return. "Sounds normal. I put my parents through hell at that age, too."

"She's adorable until she opens her mouth. And boys don't have those hormones affecting their emotions."

He chuckled. "It's different, but I think the torment is the same."

Now she chuckled. He liked the sound. It was soft and genuine.

"How long has it been since you left Honey Creek?" he asked.

"Fifteen years."

That sparked his interest. "You were around when Mark Walsh was supposedly murdered."

"Yes. I remember that."

Some of the gossips said she'd slept with him, too. He saw her lips tighten and she adjusted her grip on the steering wheel, almost as if she were preparing herself for questions; or maybe she wondered if he thought what most others thought and didn't like it.

"When was the last time you saw him?" he asked, watching her.

She gave him a warning glance. "Are you wondering if I knew where he went instead of dying like everybody thought?"

"I'll try anything if I think it might help me find his killer."

"The last time I saw him was at the post office with his wife, about a month before he died…or everyone thought he did."

"He never contacted you after that?"

"No." Her voice sounded sharper. She knew why he'd asked that question. The rumors. Could she blame him? He had no way of knowing unless he asked.

Before he could explain that, she added in the same sharp tone, "And just for the record, I didn't sleep with him."

He almost smiled at her defensiveness. He'd bet his badge that she was telling the truth. When some people lied, their defensiveness gave them away. But Lily's was driven more by vulnerability. He wondered if she knew that about herself… that she protected her vulnerability with defensiveness.

The way his interest kept intensifying the longer he spent with her made him check himself. He believed her about

Walsh, but how much of the other rumors were true? There were a lot. He didn't want to involve himself with a Jezebel. But if the talk was exaggerated…

"Is it true you danced naked in front of the market on your twenty-fifth birthday?" he asked, making sure he sounded teasing.

She gave him two quick looks as she drove, without smiling. "Trying to find out if all the gossip is true?"

"What if I was?" He was serious now, because he really wanted her to tell him.

"I'd want to know why."

"I think you know the answer to that." He looked at her suggestively. He wasn't asking in the capacity of sheriff.

She concentrated on driving. He waited for her to reply, but she didn't. Maybe she didn't like it that he'd asked. Maybe she wondered if he was like many others in Honey Creek, buying all the talk. He never took rumors to heart, but right now he wanted the truth.

"Aren't you going to answer my question?"

"Yes."

"Yes, you danced naked in front of the market?"

"And I went sailing for two weeks with a man I met in Vegas. Two of his friends went with us. I jumped from airplanes. I went on a safari in Africa and survived a hurricane in Barbados. I raced dirt bikes. I got in fights with other women. I even tried mud-wrestling." She stopped talking and he found himself absorbing everything she said. She'd left a couple of things out. "Oh, and I drank a lot of whiskey, smoked pot and broke up a couple of marriages."

Wes knew that one of the women whose husband she'd taken was still angry and not at all happy she was back in town. "The quilting group had a lot of fun with the sailing thing," he said. And the rumors were X-rated.

Lily rolled her eyes. "I heard about that group."

"Quilting's just their excuse."

He liked how that made her smile. But she didn't say any more.

"Not going to comment on the sailing thing, huh?"

"What do you want me to say? It's all true. Is that what you want to know? Is that why you're asking me all these questions? Yes, I went sailing with three men."

He stared at her. The rumors hadn't been kind. She'd gone sailing with three men and had sex with all of them. More than once.

She looked over at him, her expression matter-of-fact. She wasn't denying anything, nor did she appear ashamed. But he was pretty sure that was a cover-up. She wasn't proud of her early adulthood.

"How did the quilting group find out about that?" he asked.

"I was friends with your sister Maisie back then." She sent him a challenging look.

His older sister could get a little overbearing sometimes. "She does love a good tabloid tale."

"She tried to turn me into one."

"Sorry, but she didn't have to try very hard."

"I've changed since then," she said, sobering.

"I'm starting to see that," he said, making sure she saw he meant it.

Soft satisfaction made her eyes glow warmly and she resumed her concentration on driving.

"Why did you do it?" he asked.

"What? Behave that way?"

"Yes." He didn't want to hear any more about her sailing trip.

"You didn't grow up in my household."

Her father was a minister and her mother didn't work. "Too strict?"

"Strict. Judgmental. Relentless. Yeah. Nothing I did was good enough. So I thought it'd be neat if I showed them what bad really was."

He heard the regret in the form of sarcasm in her tone. "You wish you hadn't done the things you've done?"

"Not everything. The safari was a great experience. So was rock-climbing and jumping from planes and even sailing, except for the company I had."

Her hands adjusted on the wheel again, and now she seemed to be getting upset. He didn't want to upset her, especially since he was enjoying this, and her. He didn't question her further.

Looking ahead, he noticed they were almost at the outskirts of town.

"Will you just drop me off at the sheriff's office? I have a Jeep I use for work there. I can drive that until I take care of my SUV."

"Sure." A few minutes later, she pulled to a stop in front of his small office, a redbrick building with white trim and a sign that said Honey Creek County Sheriff.

"It'll be interesting explaining this to my deputies," he said, more to keep her from leaving before he could ask her out on a date.

"If any rumors start that I had a tryst in Deer Lodge, I'll know where it started." She smiled, but he could tell she didn't want that to happen.

"No deputy of mine would do that, and I certainly wouldn't. I'll just stick with the truth…I met this beautiful woman at Montana State Prison…."

She started laughing. Once again, the sound reached into him, this time strumming a stronger infatuation.

"Yeah, that would stir up a few questions." She grew somber as she said it.

"Nobody needs to know we met there. I'll just tell them you totaled my SUV."

He loved the flirtatious glint in her eyes. "And you can tell them I wrecked you for any other woman."

"You might have."

Her eyes blinked in response, an indication of the flurry of thoughts, and, he hoped, some warming emotions his reply had set off.

"Do you have any plans Friday night?" he asked.

Her smile came and went on her face, as if the idea first tantalized her and then made her shy away. "You're asking me out on a date?"

"Is that so hard to believe?"

"No…well, yes…I mean, you're the sheriff."

"Amazing, isn't it? Me, sheriff of Honey Creek County."

"I don't mean that. It's just…you're… And I'm…"

"I'm a man and you're a woman. Are you trying to tell me you're…" He lifted his eyebrows and let his expression finish his meaning, even though he was teasing.

"No!"

"Then go out with me. Dinner. Friday night. I'll pick you up or we can meet somewhere. Whatever you're most comfortable with."

She stared at him. And then turned and looked through the windshield.

"Come on. It'll be fun. I can already tell," he coaxed.

"I don't know…"

"I promise I'll behave."

Finally she looked at him.

"Friday night. Seven o'clock," he said.

Again, she seemed to waver between accepting and not. "I don't think now is a good time. With all the talk around town…"

"All the more reason to go out with me. It's like you said, I'm the sheriff. It'll be good for people to see you with me."

"Or bad for you to be seen with me," she countered.

"I don't care what people say. It's the truth that matters."

Her eyes grew soft with warming affection. Just what he wanted to see. He grinned. But she was going to turn him down. He could tell.

"Think about it," he said.

She smiled a little and nodded. "I will."

"Think hard." He smiled.

She laughed, as soft as the look in her eyes. Damn, he liked her.

He opened the truck door and stepped out, turning to face her. "At least I know where to find you." The library.

"Don't you dare." But her lovely smile proved she was kidding.

"See you soon, Lily Masterson."

The last thing he heard before closing the door was another warm laugh. Feeling good, he headed for the office with a little extra verve in his step.

When he reached the door, he looked back. She hadn't pulled into the street yet. She was still watching him with a soft smile. And that told him all he needed to know.

Chapter 2

"One of the boys at school asked me if I was as good as my mother."

Damn. Would it ever stop?

Lily looked across the truck at her fourteen-year-old daughter. Her blue eyes and black hair mirrored her own. May was only five-four for now, but she'd probably grow another four inches to match her height, too.

"What did you do?"

"Nothing. I walked away."

"Good girl. What comes out of people's mouths isn't important unless it's true." Realizing that's what Wes had told her, she shook off thoughts of him. "It's your actions that mean more. You show them who you are. You don't crumble."

"You're always saying that," May retorted.

"Arguing and getting into fights isn't the way to handle this."

"But it's true, what they're saying about you."

"Some of it used to be true. It isn't anymore. They'll see that eventually, as long as we don't let them beat us down."

"I don't know why you wanted to come back to this stupid town. It sucks here."

"Watch your mouth."

"Everyone thinks you're a slut."

"Well, I'm not. And I told you to watch your mouth."

"They call me a slut, too."

Lily gave up. "You aren't a slut."

"I don't have any friends because of you!"

That broke her heart in two. "You have Peri." She was a cute little redhead that May said was an outcast like her.

"Peri is a dolt."

Pulling to a stop in front of the school, Lily watched May's face go grim with dread.

"Hold your head high and do well in your classes. You'll meet some friends who won't judge you the way the others do." When May didn't move to get out of the truck, Lily said, "Go on. You're better than this, May."

May turned her head and looked at her. "I don't like it here."

"We aren't moving. We just got here."

With a heavy sigh, May opened the door and hopped out.

"I love you," Lily said.

May looked at her and didn't say anything before slamming the truck door. Lily watched her until she disappeared inside the school building, and then drove away.

That was the hardest part about all the talk in town. She hated what it was doing to May. But they'd get through it. The talk wouldn't go on forever.

She headed for Main Street. Bonnie Gene Kelley had called this morning and Lily had agreed to meet her. Parking, she got out and started walking down the street. Bonnie Gene had an uncanny ability to pry out whatever was bugging her. It had been a week since the hearing and still Lily was having trouble dealing with seeing Brandon in person.

Walking down Main Street, Lily was vaguely aware of people turning their heads to look at her. She passed the Corner Bar and jaywalked across the street toward the West Ridge Hotel. Next door was the Honey-B Café, where she'd agreed to meet Bonnie Gene. For once they weren't meeting at Kelley's Cookhouse, the restaurant Bonnie Gene and her husband ran.

Bonnie Gene was one of two people in town Lily trusted enough to call friends. She had stuck by her through everything over all these years, starting out as more of a mother figure, but as Lily grew older, their friendship had grown. She was the only person who knew about Brandon.

Lily wasn't sure if that was a good thing. As soon as Bonnie Gene discovered she'd testified at Brandon's hearing, she'd picked up on how badly it was affecting her. And Bonnie Gene didn't take no for an answer once she made her mind up about something. So, whether Lily liked it or not, which this morning she didn't, she had to meet her friend for breakfast before heading to the library for work.

The thought of eating breakfast soured her stomach. She'd just die if the parole board decided to release Brandon after the agony of her testimony. He hadn't done a very convincing job pleading his case. As far as she was concerned, he'd been cold and deliberate, stating that he'd received treatment while incarcerated and he was reformed and ready for society. He'd even had a plan. Move back to his hometown in North Carolina and work for his dad's remodeling company.

Ready for society. More like ready to hunt down more women in society. He'd just come out of a fifteen-year drought.

Surely he was eager to assuage his evil cravings. She hoped the parole board hadn't been fooled.

Pushing open the door to the café, Lily looked around for Bonnie Gene and spotted her at a table, waving a hand, her dark brown hair brushing her shoulders. For a sixty-four-year-old, she still looked good. Lily went toward her, dreading having to talk about Brandon. She sat across the table, seeing Bonnie Gene's light brown eyes soften with sympathy. Sometimes sympathy was worse than anything else. She wished people would just treat her like a normal woman.

"I'm all right," she almost snapped.

"Don't get all defensive with me," Bonnie Gene said. "I know what this is doing to you."

Lily felt her shoulders sag and she leaned back in the chair. A waitress stopped by the table.

"Nothing for me," Lily said.

"Two Western skillets," Bonnie Gene told the waitress. "And some good strong coffee."

"I'm not hungry." Especially for Honey-B's ham-and-cheese-laden Western skillet.

"You have to eat." Then to the waitress, "Two skillets."

The waitress glanced once at Lily, then scribbled the order and left. Lily wondered if that look was because of the rumors rather than Bonnie Gene's bulldozing.

"You've been doing so well up until now," Bonnie Gene said.

"I'm fine."

"There you go again, all defensive. It's okay to be upset about this, you know. Anybody would be."

"I'm over it."

"You're strong and you've done well with your life. You never let it get you down, but seeing him in person like that…"

She'd overcome the trauma of her rape, but now it felt as if she were going through it all over again. Reliving it.

"What was it like seeing him again?"

Lily angled her head with a do-you-have-to-ask look. Bonnie Gene was trying to get her to talk.

"I mean, how was he toward you?"

"Actually, he never looked at me. If I didn't know better, I'd say he seemed uncomfortable that I was there."

"Really?"

She nodded.

"What if he was?"

"He was acting." For the sake of the board.

"I've heard some criminals get that way at their parole hearings."

"That's a crock." She'd never believe Brandon was miraculously cured. Anyone who could do what he'd done to her and have no remorse couldn't possibly be normal, even after spending so long in prison. Especially after that.

Bonnie Gene looked at her for a while. She didn't have to say anything. She was still worried about Lily. "When do you find out what the parole board decides?"

"Any day now."

"No wonder you're such a mess. Not knowing must be killing you."

It was, but she'd get through it. She would.

"You sure you're going to be all right?"

"Yes." She wouldn't have it any other way. "Promise."

Bonnie Gene smiled. "You might have been a wild child before you left this place, but you were always strong. Not too many women could recover to the extent you have."

"Oh, I don't know about that. Survival is a pretty good motivator." It had been for her.

The waitress reappeared with coffee and another long look at Lily. Lily ignored her until she left, lifting the cup and taking a tentative sip. It went down all right. That was a good sign.

"Somebody told Maisie Colton that you dropped Wes off at the county sheriff's building last week."

Lily looked at Bonnie Gene. Great. Just what she needed.

"She asked him why," Bonnie Gene said.

Remembering what he'd said, she wondered if he'd stayed true to his word. She hadn't seen him around town since that day, despite all his charm in asking her out. But maybe he wasn't on a timetable. He was a man, after all. And it had only been a week.

"What did he say?" she asked.

"That you ran into him outside of town."

She couldn't help smiling. That wasn't exactly a lie. Montana State Prison *was* outside of town.

"That's what I thought," Bonnie Gene said, and Lily knew her smile had given her away. "Spill it, girlfriend."

"There's nothing to spill. I wasn't paying attention and I ran into him and wrecked his SUV so I drove him to work."

Her friend's mouth dropped open. "What? You got in a wreck? What happened?"

"I wasn't going fast, only about twenty miles an hour." Which was pretty fast in a parking lot.

"What happened?" Bonnie Gene repeated.

Lily didn't want to tell her too much. What if it got around town?

"Come on. It's me." Bonnie Gene pointed at herself and looked injured. "You ran into our hunky sheriff and you didn't even tell me."

"It was no big deal."

"Did he ask you out?"

"Bonnie Gene…"

"Oh, this is getting good. Where were you when you ran into him?"

Lily cocked her head, not wanting to talk about this. She'd much rather lie and get on with her day. But it was so hard lying to Bonnie Gene, her one true friend through everything.

The waitress returned with their food and left.

"Where?" Bonnie Gene demanded, scooping up a forkfull of eggs.

"Outside of town." She pushed her eggs around on the plate.

"Wes just said that to protect you." Lily watched Bonnie Gene's eyes and knew she was starting to figure things out.

"When did you run into him?" she asked.

"A few days ago."

"What day?" Bonnie ate more eggs, chewing and looking at her expectantly.

Darn it! "A week ago." She hesitated. "Today."

Bonnie Gene swallowed as her puzzle came together. "A week ago today? Was it the day of the parole hearing? Come to think of it, I haven't seen Wes driving his SUV since…."

"Oh, all right. It was the parking lot of the prison, okay? He doesn't know why I was there, though, so don't be spreading any rumors. I don't want anyone to know."

She set her fork down. "Honey, have I ever failed you yet?"

Lily relaxed. "No. I'm sorry."

"You're just a little rattled right now. I understand."

Before Lily could respond, a woman appeared next to their table. Her pear-shaped body was stuffed into peach-colored stretch pants and a dark purple T-shirt that clung to rolls of fat. Shoulder-length red hair framed angry pale green eyes adorned by too much makeup.

"You have a lot of nerve," she said to Lily.

Lily tried to place the woman but didn't recognize her. She looked at Bonnie Gene, who shrugged her shoulders.

"I shouldn't be surprised you don't remember me," the woman said.

Oh, no. Another piece of her past was about to rear its ugly head.

"Karen. Andy Hathaway is my husband?" The woman said it like a question.

Then memory came rushing back. A brief affair packed with lots of naked writhing at a downtown hotel. Andy Hathaway had been hung like a Hoover hose.

And, my oh, my, was she uncomfortable now. "Karen, I…" What could she possibly say? Sorry for humping your husband? But it was so long ago….

"Save it. You think anybody is glad to see you back? I don't know why you bothered."

"It's been a long time," she said, knowing it was feeble.

Sure enough, that only managed to anger Karen more. "It would be better if you left town. I never wanted to have to lay eyes on you again after what you did."

"I can understand how you feel, but—"

Karen leaned over and pointed her finger in front of Lily's face. "You don't know the first thing about how I feel."

Lily moved her head back as Karen jabbed her finger too close.

"You didn't give a rat's ass how I felt back then and you don't give a rat's ass now. I want you gone from here."

Lily wanted to tell her she was being ridiculous after so much time had passed.

"Lily's not the same as she was before she left," Bonnie Gene said.

"You stay out of this. It's none of your business."

"Karen…I don't know how to say this but…I'm sorry. I really am."

Karen's mouth tightened until her lips turned white. She picked up a glass of water from the table and tossed it toward Lily's head. Water splashed and ran down her hair and face. She wiped her eyes and looked up at Karen.

"I want you gone, you hear me?" Karen hissed, and then turned her back and marched out of the restaurant.

Still numb, Lily noticed the entire café had gone silent and everyone was staring at her.

"Does she really think she can make you leave town?" Bonnie Gene asked. "Seeing you must have really riled her."

Dabbing her face with a napkin, Lily didn't know what to say to that. She felt bad and yet…there wasn't a thing she could do. People started whispering around them.

"You ready to go?" Bonnie Gene asked.

"Yeah. Now would be good."

Bonnie Gene put down enough cash to cover their check and stood. Taking the napkin with her, Lily followed her outside, wiping the front of her shirt.

"Good thing it's just water," Bonnie Gene said.

"Yeah, it could have been a gun."

She exchanged a look with Bonnie Gene.

Lily pushed the library door open and dug in her purse for her ringing cell phone. The strap slipped down her arm, causing her to adjust her hands like a juggler. She found the phone.

"Lily Masterson?" a woman queried.

"Yes." She slung her purse strap back over her shoulder. It slipped back down to her elbow, nearly yanking the phone away from her ear.

Some days nothing ever went right.

"This is Karla Harrison from Montana State Prison?" the caller said, her inflection rising at the end.

The mention of the prison stopped Lily's breath and a tiny shock wave made her stomach turn and her heart jump into faster beats. She stopped walking.

"Yes?" She remembered the woman. The victims' officer who'd walked her to the parking lot.

"Is now a good time to talk?" Karla asked in an overly gentle tone, as if she had to walk on eggshells in order to talk to a poor, helplessly traumatized woman.

Lily hated being treated like that. She started walking again.

"Of course." This *was* turning out to be a real crapper of a day. She kicked her office door open. It bounced against the stopper and swung back toward her, tapping her arm and knocking her purse off her shoulder again.

"The parole board has reached a decision in Brandon Gates's hearing."

Now consumed with apprehension, Lily walked to her desk and sat down, letting her purse slip to the floor beside her chair. "Yes?"

"I'm sorry to have to tell you this, but they've decided to release him. You'll be getting a letter in the mail."

"You're *releasing* him?" How could they?

"It was the board's decision."

Apprehension morphed into outrage. "What did they base it on?" Prison overpopulation?

"He went through treatment while he was incarcerated and according to the board, has a valid plan for reentering society."

"Plan?" she all but shouted. *Valid plan?* It was maddening. "What plan? A rapist tells you he's moving to North Carolina and that's enough for you to set him free?"

"The board is very careful when they make decisions like this, Lily. Please try and understand that. They wouldn't have released him if they didn't think he'd do his best to stay rehabilitated."

"I don't believe for one minute that he's *rehabilitated*." A hundred images assailed her, all of them from the endless hours she'd spent in that cabin. Tears burned her eyes.

"I'm sorry, Ms. Masterson. I know this is hard for you. If you'd like I can give you the name of a good counselor near your home town."

"I don't need a *counselor*," Lily snapped. "Stop talking to me like that."

"I'm sorry, Ms. Masterson, I—"

"When?" Lily swallowed the lump of hurt in her throat.

"Excuse me?"

"When will he be released?"

"Next week. Friday. It's all in the letter."

Lily never hung up on anyone, but today she did. She ended the call and held the phone in her palm, staring down at it, shaking, lost in a maelstrom of old pain and a deep sense of injustice.

She wiped a tear that had slipped from her eye.

There was no punishment that would change what she'd endured, both during her assault and after. The month that followed it had been the worst, with no one to turn to and nowhere to go that felt like home. No wonder she'd tried to obliterate the experience with a one-night stand. It wouldn't have been her first.

Having sex with a stranger had been a mistake, an attempt to somehow minimize what had happened to her. Instead, that last wild night—like so many she'd had before her rape—had done the opposite. It had made her feel dirty and cheap and had thrown her into a severe state of depression.

Hearing a sound, she looked up to see Emily, her assistant, standing in the doorway. She blinked her eyes clear.

"You okay?" her assistant asked with a worried frown.

"Yes. Fine." Lily held up the phone. "Just a personal call."

Emily didn't look convinced. "We got a couple of boxes of books from a donor yesterday."

"Good. Let's get going on sorting them." She could use the distraction right now. Putting her phone down, she stood and moved around the desk.

Brandon Gates was going to be released. It didn't seem real. It was so unfair.

"They're all romance novels. I don't think we have enough room for all of them."

Lily forced a smile. "We won't keep them all. Just the ones in good condition." She passed Emily and headed out into the main library.

Karla's news hung inside her like low, dreary fog. It was what she'd been dreading since the hearing. Her worst fear had come true. Would he really go to North Carolina? Or would he risk going back to prison to come and find her? That would be very stupid, unless he thought he could get away with it. Lily had to smother a shiver with the thought of him finding her. And she hated that, her reaction, what he was still capable of doing to her.

Did he know she'd lived in Honey Creek back then? She'd never told him that night, but maybe he found out later. Did he know she'd moved back?

"Are you sure you're all right?" Emily asked.

Lily had forgotten her assistant had followed her. "Yeah." She bent to pick up a few books from the first box and turned to place them on a table in alphabetical order by author name.

"Who were you just talking to?"

She sent a look over at Emily, letting her know she was prying too much.

"Sorry," Emily said.

The sound of someone behind them made Lily turn. So did Emily.

Wes Colton stood on the other side of the boxes, holding a book in his hand. The sight of him stole her breath and shards of excitement chased her bleakness away.

"Looks like you got some new inventory." His voice was masculine and as appealing as she remembered. Maybe more so.

What was he doing here? Her insurance company was handling the transaction with his SUV. Of course, he had another reason, but she wasn't sure she was ready to face that.

"Wes." She hoped she didn't sound as schoolgirlish as she thought.

Emily glanced from her back to Wes.

He held up the book, the picture of a bare-chested man looking down at the soulful face of a brunette. "Interesting cover art."

Lily snatched the book from his hand and dropped it back into the box he'd taken it from. "It's popular fiction."

He didn't say anything, just grinned his amusement and something else. Was he flirting with her?

"Uh...I'll go help at the checkout counter," Emily said, smiling secretively as she wandered off.

Uncomfortable with the way Emily left them alone and the realization that she'd picked up on Wes's flirting, too, Lily had to force herself to look at him.

"How are you?" she asked.

"Good. You?" Was he nervous, too, or was this small talk a way for him to get a conversation going?

"Good," she played along.

He smiled wider. "I came by to see you."

His announcement dispelled the awkwardness. Gladness expanded and bloomed in her chest.

"I bought a new vehicle in Bozeman yesterday," he added.

"Oh, that's good. I hope you like it as much as your last SUV."

"More so. Cost me a little more than I expected, but it's worth it." His gaze floated over her face. "It's good to see you again."

Another charge of excitement tickled her. She smiled and saw how he noticed. "It's good to see you, too."

Losing herself as she met his smiling eyes, feeling his attraction match her own, it took her a moment to realize how they were behaving. She glanced around. Emily was busy with someone at the checkout counter. There was no one standing near them. No one had noticed them ogling each other.

Reality came down a little harder. Did she really want to encourage Wes? Aside from the folly of him getting involved with what everyone considered the town floozy, she would be no good for any man right now.

The news of her rapist's release had robbed her of her strength. She was vulnerable again. The same struggle she'd overcome so many years ago was returning. Would she be able to go home and not feel as though she had to lock every door and window and double-check them periodically? She hated that kind of weakness, the power Brandon Gates still had over her. Would she ever be free of that part of her life? It was disheartening.

No. She refused to succumb to irrational fears. He was moving back to North Carolina. That was far away from here, and he'd be foolish to try and make contact with her again. He had to know she'd expose him if he did.

"Don't worry, our secret is still safe," Wes said.

He'd given her a brief distraction from her troubles, but they weren't going to magically go away. "You shouldn't have come here."

"Would you rather we go back to the prison?"

He was trying be funny, but he had no way of knowing how upsetting the reference was for her. She looked down at the floor.

Wes was quiet for a few beats. "So…how do you like the library?"

Back to safe topics. He had a way of easing her into those and keeping her enchanted.

She glanced around at the dark wood shelves and Emily helping someone else now at the checkout counter. Something about this place made her feel good. It soothed her. Maybe it was her love of books. They'd installed new computers a few months ago. Some of the floor had been carpeted and some refinished with new hardwood. New lighting had been installed, too. It was cozy. Fresh. Clean and bright. "I like it." She looked back at him. "I like the work, too."

"How long have you been doing this line of work? I never got a chance to ask you that when you drove me to my office."

"I went to college after I left Honey Creek. It's been about ten years now." He was doing a good job of taking her mind off that phone call, drawing her out of darkness and into the light of his purpose in coming to see her. The Sheriff of Honey Creek County was interested in her.

"It suits you."

Did it? She took in his chest in his sheriff uniform, his height, and even though he was flirting, he had a commanding presence.

"Being sheriff suits you." She couldn't believe she'd said it. "I mean—"

"I know what you mean," he cut her off. "And I like that."

Oh, boy…

"Why did you leave the navy?" she asked, more to divert the conversation.

"I wanted to come home."

"You planned on running for sheriff?"

"Not at first."

"What did you do in the navy, anyway?" How had he gone from that to law enforcement?

He hesitated and the glint of infatuation left his eyes. She wondered if this was a sore subject.

"I joined the SEALs."

Her brow rose. She couldn't help it. "Wow. You passed that training?"

Was he studying her? He seemed as though he was suspicious of her. Did he wonder why she'd asked? Why did it matter?

"I worked with a team for a while," he finally answered, "but I didn't like the travel."

"And the danger?" Did he like that?

"That didn't bother me so much. I was careful."

Careful? "You sound so confident."

"You have to be."

"Is being sheriff of this little town enough of a stimulus for you?"

"I was young when I joined the SEALs. I don't need adrenaline rushes to stay interested anymore. So, yes, I like what I do now. And there's a lot to be said about dodging fewer bullets."

"You've dodged bullets in Honey Creek?"

"In a manner of speaking."

And he'd dodged them as a SEAL. "Didn't you like being a SEAL?" He was sure acting strange about it.

"I liked it. I just wanted to come home," he answered curtly.

She decided not to question him further on that. He obviously didn't want to talk about it.

"When is your brother going to be released?" she asked instead.

A woman looked at them as she passed. Lily wondered if she'd heard what she'd asked.

Wes didn't appear to notice, in fact, his tension eased. "I should have the court order in the next week or two."

"That's great."

She could only imagine what it would be like to watch your brother spend so much time in prison for something he didn't do. There would have to be some kind of effect on Damien. It had to have changed him somehow. Hardened him. Would he be dangerous?

She didn't want to find out. Instead of continuing to question Wes, she steered clear of the more detailed questions she was dying to ask.

"You must have been pretty young when he was convicted."

"Eighteen."

"Is that why you joined the SEALs?" Did he want to learn how to fight? To kill? Had he planned to go after whoever was responsible for wrongly convicting his brother?

He took a moment to answer and she inwardly kicked herself for asking. She hadn't meant to bring that up again.

"It might have had something to do with it. I never stopped believing Damien was innocent. I didn't know what to do. Maybe I joined the SEALs because it gave me a sense of control, whereas with Damien's situation, I've never had control."

"Even though you wanted it."

"Yes."

"I think everyone does the things they do in life for a reason, whether they know it or not."

"You became a librarian for a particular reason?"

"I love to read."

"Is that the only reason?"

She had to stop herself from fidgeting. She'd admitted to no one what had led her down this path. "It's what pointed me in that direction."

"When did you start reading a lot?"

"It wasn't until later, after...after I left." Now she was getting really uncomfortable.

"It was probably a good thing you did leave."

She just looked at him. If only he knew.

"I mean so you could find something to do with your life."

Did he mean other than being a wild woman?

"Without the pressure of..." He seemed at a loss for words.

"I should really get back to work."

He looked at her a moment. "Scared you away again, huh?"

"No, it's not that." What a lie that was. Brandon's release was hurtling her back in time. How could she have a normal relationship with any man if every reminder made her feel vulnerable?

"Then have dinner with me. Tonight. What time do you get off?"

"Oh...that's sweet, but...it's just not a good time."

"You're shooting me down again." He said it playfully.

"I'm afraid so." She couldn't help laughing. "Besides, did you know I'm forty?"

"Wow, your life is over."

She shook her head. "You're only thirty-three."

"Word gets around. You're old enough to be my sister."

"Stop that." But she laughed.

He grinned and she got the distinct impression that he

wasn't about to give up on her. There was something appealing about that. There was something appealing about a man who wasn't afraid of rejection. It showed boundless ambition and self-confidence. A humble ego.

There was a time in her life when she would have jumped headfirst into a relationship with a younger man, but things had changed.

He backed away. "I'll be back."

"People are going to talk," she said.

Emily had finished with the person at the counter and now watched them.

"Let them." He backed up some more.

She wasn't so sure, but his teasing was infectious. "Easy for you to say."

He took another step back. "It'll give them something else to talk about besides you."

"Oh, yeah? How do you figure that?"

"I just got a bug in me to start reading more."

Meaning he'd be stopping by the library more often. Her first reaction was to tell him no, but the delight he'd made her feel stopped her. She didn't try to sway him.

Wes left the library wondering if he'd misread the back-and-forth emotions from Lily. Sometimes she flirted with him and at other moments she withdrew. Was it their age difference? He wasn't that much younger than her. And she had good skin. Hell, he'd probably look older than her when he was forty.

He'd been trying to contact the victims' officer ever since the morning after Lily had plowed into his truck. She'd seemed to know Lily so he'd called a friend he'd made over the years Damien had been incarcerated and asked for her contact information. The minute he learned she was a victims' officer, he'd gotten more interested in finding out the real reason Lily had gone to the prison. But the officer had gone on a weeklong vacation the day after Lily had wrecked his SUV. He'd planned to wait to go to the library until after he spoke with her, but the truth was, he couldn't stay away any longer. What if Lily started thinking he wasn't interested?

He just hoped she wasn't messed up with an inmate at Montana State Prison. She said she'd changed but...

It'd been a week. He'd call the victims' officer again.

He drove to the west side of town and pulled to a stop in front of the Honey Creek County Sheriff's office. Getting out, he walked into the building, passing the front counter and heading to his office directly behind that, and sat behind his desk. He leaned back and let himself stare at nothing for a while, thinking about Lily. Maybe he should start to worry about how much he was beginning to like her.

The legal pad on his desk caught his eye. It was full of scribbled notes about Mark Walsh's murder case. He'd jotted them down earlier. Some were centered around the money-laundering angle the FBI was investigating, others were on the note found on the body of the man who murdered Jake Pierson's partner. Jake was the first FBI agent assigned to the money-laundering investigation and Jim Willis had been his partner. Since this whole thing started, Wes had gotten to know both of them. Jim had been a good friend to both him and Jake. He shouldn't have died like that, shot by a hit man who was after Jake for information the investigation had uncovered.

The note found on Jake's partner's body hadn't been signed, but it was on a special kind of stationary that had bothered Wes ever since he'd seen it. The stationary was expensive. Not just anyone would use it. He'd been all over town tracking down possible sources. One lead had taken him to the Colton ranch, where he'd found some in his dad's office. Was that significant? Probably not. The stationary could have been ordered from an office-supply catalog. Anyone could have ordered some. It would be tough narrowing down a suspect that way. And of course, there were no prints on the paper other than those belonging to the hit man.

A knock on the open door brought his head up. Deputy Ryan King stood there. He was a six-foot lean-framed man with fine, light brown hair whose light green eyes kept the women coming around, but he never strayed from his wife.

"Come in," Wes said.

Ryan closed the door and moved closer to Wes's desk. "Sorry to bother you, Sheriff. I'm not one to give gossip much thought, but my wife told me something I thought you'd want to hear."

Leaning back in his chair, Wes waited.

"She goes to that quilting group that meets in town. You know the one?"

"Yes. What about it?"

"Well, Terri said there was talk about you and that Masterson woman spending time together. Someone saw her drop you off here at the office and said you looked like you were getting along really well."

How long before it got around he'd just left the library? Wes chuckled. Didn't those women have anything better to do than talk about people?

"Some people take offense to you getting messed up with someone like her," Ryan said. "You're the law in this town. If people don't respect you.…"

"It's been fifteen years since Lily left this town."

"That doesn't matter. It's your integrity in question."

"She isn't the same person. She's grown-up now. People will see that after a while."

"But if you continue to see her…"

Now he was beginning to get annoyed. "It's just talk."

"People are wondering where you were with her, where you could have met her."

"It doesn't matter how or where I met her." He looked pointedly up at his deputy. "I could have met her anywhere in town before that."

"I'm sorry, I know it's none of my business. It's just…your reputation."

"I'll worry about my own reputation, but thanks for letting me know."

"Come time for reelection…"

Wes looked up from the pile of papers on his desk and lifted his brow.

Ryan frowned, but relented.

When his deputy had left, Wes couldn't focus on the mound of work he had to do. Maybe he should pay more attention to what the town was saying. What if something got around that would hurt Lily? What harm would it be to use Ryan as a way of monitoring the gossip? He didn't care what was being said, but Lily did. And that was reason enough for him.

He picked up his phone and dialed Ryan's extension.

Chapter 3

"You've got one of the best pair of blue eyes I've ever seen." Levi Garrison came into step beside her. "Has anyone ever told you that?"

May Masterson rolled those blue eyes that were so like her mother's and didn't slow down on her way to her next class. Levi easily kept up with her. He was tall and had a long stride.

"I'm serious. I meant to tell you that the other day."

"When you were making fun of my mother?" Jerk.

"Yeah, well, about that…"

"Say anything smart and I'll knock your front teeth out," she said without looking at him. He was one of the most popular boys in eleventh grade. He was a football player and active on committees. He was smart, too, but not as smart as her. May knew her GPA was higher than this yokel's.

"I've been meaning to apologize for that. You took it all wrong anyway."

"How else am I supposed to take it when someone asks me if I'm as good as my mother?"

"That wasn't me. I didn't say that."

"No, you said I was prettier."

"You are."

She sent him a glare.

"You took it wrong. I wasn't after you that way."

"You said I had a nicer tail."

"I was just havin' fun. Who cares if your mom was easy when she was in high school? That was a long time ago."

May stopped and curled her hand into a fist. She raised it and brought it back for good momentum.

Levi caught it as she began to swing. Her fist fit into his hand.

His green eyes flared with something hot. "I'm sorry, okay? I didn't mean to make you mad."

"What do you care?"

He made the mistake of letting his gaze fall to her chest before meeting her eyes again.

She pushed him with her free hand. "Leave me alone, you jerk!"

"Hey." He let go of her fist. "I'm trying to be friends here."

"I don't want any friends." Not here anyway. She missed her friends in Sacramento. No one called her a slut there.

She pivoted and marched down the hall again, dodging other students, bumping someone's shoulder. A girl narrowed her eyes at her as they passed each other. May flipped her off.

Levi took hold of her wrist and pulled her to the side of the hall, twirling her smoothly. Her back came against a locker, but not hard at all. Levi was agile in the way he handled her. She didn't want to like that about him.

He put his hand on the locker above and beside her head and leaned closer. "I said I was sorry."

Her breath got stuck in her throat.

He leaned back and offered his hand. She looked down at it and back up at his cute face.

"What do you want?"

"Your friendship."

"That sounds like a line." Except he seemed sincere. Wouldn't it be great if one of the most popular boys in school liked her? "What do you really want?"

"To take you out. But that can wait. I'll settle for being friends for now."

"And once we're friends? Then what? You try to get into my panties?"

"No. I'm not after you like that, I told you."

"I don't believe you." But she wanted to.

"Just start by taking my hand. If all you can offer is hello in the halls, that's fine by me."

She eyed his hand again. What harm would it be to accept his apology? She could be reasonable. It felt good to have someone on her side for a change.

But what if he wasn't? What if he was just playing her? What if this was some kind of joke?

"Come on. I won't do anything drastic. I promise."

Deciding to give him a chance, she gave him her hand. He grinned as he shook her hand.

"You're gonna be late to class," he said, still smiling as he strolled down the emptying hall.

She watched until he disappeared into a classroom and then started to turn to head for hers.

"What do you think you're doing?"

May stopped and saw Sherilynn McTeague and one of her friends standing nearby. Sherilynn had long, blond hair and light brown eyes. She was a pretty girl in a prissy sort of way, and, like Levi, one of the most popular kids in school. But not so bright academically.

She was also Levi's girlfriend.

"Last I checked this was a public school," May said. She wasn't afraid of this prom queen.

"You stay away from Levi."

"Yeah," chimed in her friend, a slightly chunky, short-haired girl with big cheeks. "Go find your own boyfriend."

"Levi isn't my boyfriend. We were just talking. Not that it's any of your business." May turned to walk to her classroom.

"Careful how you talk to me, ho," Sherilynn called to her back.

Anger fired up in May like wind over a brush fire. *Ho?* Slowly, she pivoted, tensing as she moved closer to the two.

"If you're looking to get laid, do it with somebody else," the girl continued. "There are plenty of other boys who'd love to oblige you."

"Yeah," her chubby friend said. "Like mother like daughter. Isn't that what they say about people like you?"

Stopping, May's temper flared hotter. She was sick of *holding her head high* and not reacting to these unwarranted barbs like her mom always told her to do. She'd hold her head high all right. *After* she kicked both of these girly-girls' behinds.

Fisting her hand, she slugged the chubby girl right on the mouth. The girl's head jerked to the side and she stumbled backward, nearly losing her balance. See if she talked nasty ever again.

Sherilynn shoved May against one shoulder. May had to take a step back, but now she turned her attention to this girl. She swung her fist again, catching the side of her head. Then she hit lower, aiming for the soft part of her stomach. Sherilynn grunted and pulled May's hair. May yelled and slapped her hard across her cheek. Sherilynn stumbled and bumped into the chubby girl, tripping over her feet and falling. May stepped over her, meaning to straddle her and keep hitting, but the chubby girl pulled her by the arm. May yanked free and backhanded the girl on her nose. The girl retreated with a screech and held her bleeding nose.

Sherilynn was starting to sit up and climb to her feet. May lifted her foot and planted it against her chest, shoving her back to the floor. Then she straddled her and started slugging. See if she smiled pretty for any guy for a while….

The chubby girl pulled her off just as May spotted a teacher charging toward them.

"All right, in the principal's office. Now!" the teacher yelled. "All three of you!"

Sherilynn got to her feet, holding her side with one hand and her face with the other. "She started it!"

"Yeah, she hit me first," the chubby girl said.

"Is that true?" the teacher asked.

"Yeah. They were calling me names! I'm not a whore!"

"You're just like your slutty mother," Sherilynn said.

May lunged for her again.

The teacher stepped in her way, though, so all May could do was glare at the girl around her shoulder. "Wait 'til after school. I'll finish you off."

"May Masterson." The teacher grabbed both her shoulders. "You will stop this right now!"

"Make *them* stop. I didn't do anything wrong."

"Fighting isn't the answer."

"Her mom fought all the time," the chubby girl said snidely.

"How would you know, you weren't here," May retorted.

"No, but my mom was. She told me everything."

"My mom isn't like that anymore. You need to mind your own damn business."

"May, you don't swear in this school."

She zeroed in on the teacher's gaze. "Tell them to back off then."

"Why don't you tell the principal to do that." Moving one of her hands to May's elbow, she held tight and walked her down the hall, saying over her shoulder, "You girls are coming, too. Follow me."

Three days after seeing Lily, Wes walked into the West End Café in Deer Lodge, Montana. He'd searched for Karla Harrison, the victims' officer who'd come out of the prison after Lily had wrecked his SUV and had finally gotten hold of her. Once he told her who he was, she'd agreed to meet him here. She remembered him, but more importantly, she remembered Lily. He could tell she genuinely cared about her and was sure that was the only reason she was meeting him.

A few other tables were filled and talking joined the sound of dishes clanking and workers busy in the kitchen. The wood tables and chairs were scratched with age and the blue linoleum floor needed updating, and he was sure some women liked the lacy white valances above the front windows but he thought they could go with the floor.

The entry door opened and Karla walked into the small café. When he'd called her he'd asked if she'd meet him here rather than the prison. He didn't want anyone to know what he was doing, least of all Lily.

When she saw him, recognition showed on her face and she headed for his table.

"Sheriff Colton?" she asked.

He stood and took her hand in a shake. "Thanks for meeting me."

She sat down. "I have to admit, you have me curious. You didn't really say why you wanted to talk about Lily."

He sat across from her. "She's grown important to me since the accident."

Karla smiled softly. "I could tell there was something going on there." Then she sobered. "She seemed like such a strong woman when I first met her. I thought she'd do all right going to that parole hearing all by herself, but I could tell it was hard on her afterward."

There it was, the missing piece. "What parole hearing?"

"Oh...I thought you knew." Her expression turned worried. The waitress came and he ordered coffee. So did Karla, but in an absentminded way.

"Lily told me she went to the prison to see a friend," he reminded her when the waitress left.

"Oh," Karla hedged. "Yes, I remember."

"I could tell that wasn't the truth."

"I see." She poured sugar into her coffee and stirred. "I thought she'd have told you by now."

"She hasn't. I think it's too difficult for her. I was hoping you could tell me the real reason she was there."

Stopping her spoon, Karla stared at him, her hesitance etched over her expression. "I'm not sure how much I should tell you. What if she doesn't want me to?"

"Like I said, she's grown important to me. I want to help if I can."

Slowly Karla's expression smoothed. "That's very kind of you, Sheriff."

"If you aren't comfortable talking to me, you can give me the name of the inmate case manager."

He watched her process that. He was a sheriff. He had his ways of finding out what he needed with or without her help. Now that he knew Lily had gone to a parole hearing, and what day, he wouldn't have much trouble tracking down the case manager.

"No, no need for that. Lily's one of those special victims to me. A real fighter when all's said and done. I care about what happens to her, and I would love to know that she's happy. You want to know why she was there that day? She testified at Brandon Gates's parole hearing. She was the only victim who had the nerve to come forward out of all those women who testified at his trial."

Wes didn't like where this was heading. *Out of all those women…*

"Who is Brandon Gates? What was he in for?" he asked, fearing he already knew.

"Sexual assault."

"He raped her?" He supposed he shouldn't be surprised, as wary as Lily was around him, and as reluctant as she was to go out with him. Being with men had to be hard for her. Trusting them even harder.

Karla nodded. "It's so sad working with some of those women. And then the ones who seem so strong come along, like Lily, and you think they'll be all right, but…"

"When did that happen?" His mind raced to catch up. She'd left the area so long ago.

"Fifteen years ago, I think."

He could only stare at Karla. No wonder Lily had run into him with her truck. It must have killed her going to that hearing and having to face the man who'd hurt her so seriously so long ago. Surely she hadn't seen him since the trial. It must have brought it all back.

I was just visiting a friend, she'd said. That meant she didn't want anyone to know why she'd gone to the prison. It also meant she was ashamed of it. Why?

May was fourteen. He inwardly cursed. What she must have gone through if a rapist had fathered her child…

"You care about her."

His focus returned to Karla, but he decided not to answer her. "Was he released?"

Her eyes grew sad. "Yes."

It explained so much. "Where is he now?"

"He has family in North Carolina. One of the guards told me he was going to live there and stay with his brother. Apparently, his father has a remodeling company."

He nodded. Good. He was far away from here.

The waitress came to refill the coffee and he sipped.

"What happened?" It was a question he didn't want to ask, but had to. He needed to know. If he wanted to see Lily, he had to know what he was dealing with. She might be the first genuine woman he'd met in a long time. What kind of cruel irony would it be to discover she couldn't get past her tragic experience?

"She was out drinking with a friend one night. The friend went home with someone, a man. Brandon Gates abducted Lily in the parking lot and drove her to a remote cabin, and…"

He was glad she didn't elaborate. "How did she get away?"

"Late that night, she got free of the rope he used to tie her and left him sleeping. She hiked ten miles down the mountain to a main road and got help."

It took real grit to do something like that. Hike in the dark after being raped. Survival instinct had to have taken over, but not many women would be able to do something like that. She must have had experience in the back country before. Probably followed a stream or found her direction with the moon or stars. Given all the stories he'd heard about her adventurous escapades, he wasn't the least surprised.

Maybe he did have a shot with her after all. She was certainly brave enough.

"You'd be good for her."

Wes emerged from thought to look at Karla. He appreciated

her concern for Lily and her devotion to her job, but this was getting too personal.

"You being sheriff and all," Karla went on. "She'd feel safe with a man like you."

As corny as that sounded, he had to agree.

Lily walked into the main office of the high school and went to the counter where a woman waited.

"Are you May's mother?"

"Yes." She couldn't believe this. She was so angry she could spit.

"Right this way."

Lily followed the woman down a short hall just past the counter and entered the principal's office. The short-haired blonde woman in her fifties behind the desk looked up at her with obvious disdain. May sat in a chair in front of the desk. She looked sullen, causing Lily to check her anger.

The principal didn't smile. "Have a seat."

Lily sat in the chair next to May.

"They started it," May said right off the bat.

Lily pointed at her. "You be quiet." Then to the principal, "What happened?"

"Your daughter got into a fight with two other girls over a boy."

"That isn't true!"

Lily snapped a look at her daughter. May saw it and pursed her lips before looking away.

"They argued. May hit a girl named Brit Andrews first and they started to fight. Sherilynn McTeague tried to stop her but May hit her, too. Broke Brit's nose. Her mother is contemplating pressing charges."

"They called me a ho," May cut in.

Lily sent her daughter a warning look before turning back to the principal. "Is that true? Did they call her names?"

"They claim they didn't."

"That is a stinking lie!" May shouted.

"May?"

May sulked, her mouth downturned and her gaze dropping to the principal's desk.

Lily turned back to the principal. "So you've questioned the other girls?" It was all she could do not to get in the woman's face. But she didn't want to exacerbate May's situation and start another round of gossip about how her daughter was following her mother's footsteps.

"Yes."

"And what disciplinary action have you taken with them?"

"She let them go," May snarled, eyes on fire again.

"I suspended them," the principal corrected, eyeing May with impatience.

"As if that's going to stop them," May sneered.

Lily ignored her daughter's outbursts. At least the other girls were being reprimanded. But May had thrown the first punch. What kind of punishment did the principal have in mind and how much of it would be influenced by Lily's reputation?

She looked down at her daughter. "How many times have I told you not to get violent?"

"What am I supposed to do? Let them call me names and taunt me? No! I'm not going to anymore." She'd leaned over the arm of her chair, putting her face defiantly closer to Lily's.

Lily saw May's passion and decided to table the argument for now. She didn't really blame May for being upset, but she had to learn to do things the right way.

She turned to the principal. "I'm really sorry about this. I'll discipline her myself."

"I'm considering expulsion."

Lily lowered her head, feeling rage and disappointment. She wanted to tear into this biased woman for not understanding what prompted May to fight back. And she wished May would have shown more decorum. The worst part was that Lily could relate to her daughter's predicament. The familiarity stung. She'd been in this type of situation so many times. She'd deserved her punishments, and May was in danger of following the same path.

She slid her gaze to her daughter, who met it with another flash of defiance, but that quickly turned to contrition, as if she'd seen how this was affecting her mother.

Lily looked at the principal. "I'm asking you to give us one more chance. Just one. I'll work with May. She's having a hard time adjusting, that's all. This won't happen again."

"It will if they keep getting in my face about the way you were when you lived here before!" May retorted. "They think I'm the same way. I'm sick of taking it."

"We've talked about this."

"They're mean to me!"

Lily turned back to the principal. "Please."

The woman met her eyes for a while and Lily could see her seriously considering what to do. Here the woman was, staring the town Jezebel in the face, thinking she was raising another one, and thinking she should come down hard enough so that it made a solid enough impression on May that she wouldn't do this again.

"May is nothing like I was when I went to school here, and after," Lily said. "She knows better. She'll come around. Please give us another chance. All I'm asking for is one. If she does it again, I'll expel her myself."

The principal's eyes blinked but Lily saw how they softened. She waited.

"All right," she finally said. "One more chance. I gave the other girls a week of suspension. May will have the same."

Lily sighed and sank back against her chair.

"That is so unfair," May said.

"You can go now," the principal said.

May stood up with all the attitude of a slighted teenager and marched out the door ahead of Lily.

Lily followed more slowly, reaching her truck after May, who now stood at the passenger door with her arms folded, glaring at her mother. Lily felt worry slither through her.

Oh, God. What would she do if her daughter rebelled to the extent she had? She'd been so careful to raise her with an open mind, not the way her parents had raised her. Had she miscalculated somehow?

She climbed into the truck and waited before starting the engine.

"You don't get it."

Lily took in her daughter's fiery blue eyes. She had to get through to her somehow. "May, do you realize you're acting exactly the way the other kids expect you to?"

That only seemed to inflame her further. "What did you do when you went to school? When everyone called you names, what did you do?"

"I fought and got suspended. More than once."

"See?"

"See what? The answer to this isn't fighting. It didn't do me any good getting into fights and it didn't stop the talk. If anything, it made it worse."

"I'm not going to end up like you, but I can't let those girls walk all over me, either. They won't stop unless I make them."

"May…"

"You want me to be a wimp."

"No, I don't. I want you to be mature. You can't *make* anyone think the way you want them to. They'll form their own opinions no matter how many times you punch them in the nose."

"See? You don't get it."

Lily sighed, struggling to come up with something to say that would reach her.

"I'm not going to sleep around and go wild like everybody says you did," May said.

"No, but you're going to slug your way through high school and end up with a bad reputation anyway."

"I already have a bad reputation. Just being your daughter does that."

Lily had to catch her breath. That hurt so much. She'd worried coming back here would stir up talk, but she'd hoped it would fade as soon as they saw her working at the library and not going out to the bars and out with lots of men or on wild adventure trips.

She started the engine and began driving.

"I'm sorry."

Surprise made her glance at May, who met her brief look with the apology still in her eyes. It touched Lily. Maybe there was hope after all.

"I know you aren't like that anymore."

"Promise me you won't get into any more fights. If for nothing else, at least to prevent an expulsion."

May turned her face toward the window as Lily drove toward home.

"May?"

She looked at her but didn't say anything.

"I won't tolerate your being expelled from school. Do you understand that?"

"Yes."

"Then no more fights."

"Okay."

"Okay" wasn't a promise, but that was all she'd get for now. Lily knew her daughter. She just hoped May would have the good sense to listen to her.

Chapter 4

Wes left his office after talking on the phone with the new FBI agent assigned to their money-laundering investigation. The agent worked remotely and had an informant somewhere in town. Wes had tried to get him to say who that was, but he'd made a song and dance about needing to protect his informant. Wes was the sheriff. Did the agent really think he'd jeopardize the investigation? The agent was keeping the informant secret for a reason. Safety was one thing, but there was more to it than that. The agent wanted an ace in the hole, which meant the identity of the informant would come as a surprise to everyone. Maybe that person was someone prominent in town, someone everyone knew. Someone who could do a lot of damage or cause a scandal. And in Honey Creek, that meant it could be just about anyone.

What Wes wouldn't give to have Jake Pierson back on the case. But Jake had his own issues to deal with, the best one being his wife, Mary. Mary was one of Mark Walsh's daughters and had a vested interest in finding her father's killer. Mary and Jake had fallen in love when he was working the investigation, which ran into a few problems when Walsh was murdered.

Walsh was supposed to contact Jake with information about a potential money-laundering operation at Walsh Enterprises, but someone had gotten to him first. Jake had tapped into computers at the company, but nothing conclusive had turned up. Who was behind it? Now that Walsh was dead for good this time, they might never know. Jake had gotten close, but his and Mary's probing had led to his partner's death. And losing Jake's partner was a hard blow to everyone close to the investigation.

Wes climbed into his Jeep and started driving. All he needed was a break, just one big break. Some clue that would tell him who was behind Walsh's murder. He had a hunch that the murders of Jake's partner and Mark Walsh were connected to something big enough to make Mark disappear. Maybe it was the money-laundering operation. He was hoping the new agent and his informant would be able to shed some light on that. And soon.

But Wes's call to the new agent had produced nothing new on the money-laundering operation. He was tired of all the dead ends he'd encountered since finding out Mark Walsh had been murdered—for real this time.

His cell phone rang.

He put the BlackBerry to his ear. "Wes."

"Sheriff," one of his deputies said. "We got a call from Jolene Walsh this morning. She wants to meet you."

"Did she say why?"

"No. She insists on meeting with you personally. Only you."

Jolene had been among those he'd considered potential suspects, but there was nothing concrete to connect her to

Mark's murder. She'd been married to Walsh before he'd vanished fifteen years ago, and he hadn't been a model husband.

"Tell her to meet me at the office in two hours."

"She asked me to tell you to come to her house as soon as possible. Like now."

"She just wants me to drop everything and come to talk to her? Did she say why?"

"Only that it had something to do with Mark Walsh, and she's afraid to come to you because she doesn't want Mark's killer to get suspicious of her."

That made him take his foot off the gas pedal. "Did she say anything else?"

"No."

"All right. I'm on my way."

He turned onto a side street off Main and turned around. As he came to the stop sign at Main, he saw Lily enter the Honey-B Café. He checked the clock on his stereo. A little past noon. Impulse took over. It had been days since he'd seen her.

What harm would it be to make Jolene wait about an hour?

He parked on the street and walked toward the café.

Opening the restaurant's door, Wes searched inside for Lily. She was at the checkout counter and the cashier was handing her some change.

"It'll be just a few minutes," the cashier said.

"Why don't you make that two?" Wes asked, stopping the cashier midturn.

"Afternoon, Sheriff. What kind of dressing would you like with your salmon salad?"

Anything other than a salad would have worked. He looked at Lily, whose blue eyes blinked up at him. He turned back to the cashier. "Make that a Philly with cheese."

The cashier grinned. "You want that to go, too?"

He looked back at Lily, who still seemed surprised to see him…or was she happy to see him and trying to cover it up?

"Why don't you stay and join me?" he asked.

Her eyebrows lifted. "Uh…I—I was going to take it back to the library."

"I'm sure the library will be fine without you for an hour. Come on. There's a table over by the window."

She looked there.

He turned to the cashier. "Will you have our lunch brought to us over there?"

The cashier sent Lily a disapproving glance before turning back to Wes with a stiff smile. "Of course." No doubt she was miffed that the sheriff of Honey Creek County was cavorting with the likes of Lily Masterson.

Wes wondered if his lunch with Lily would make it around to the quilting group. He stepped aside and held his arm out, indicating her to precede him, hoping she would. She hesitated, but—much to his satisfaction—walked toward the table.

Sitting across from her, he watched how she quietly analyzed him.

"You don't give up easily, do you?" she asked.

"Not when it matters."

That won him a soft smile. "Don't you have work to do?"

"Yeah, but it's lunchtime. A sheriff's got to eat just like everybody else."

"So you just happened to decide to come here for lunch?"

He liked the flirty light in her eyes. "Are you wondering if I followed you?"

She fiddled with the cardboard menu display in the middle of the table. "Did you?"

He chuckled. "No. I was driving out of town after a call from my deputy, and I turned around to head the other way when I saw you."

Setting aside the cardboard display, she said, "So you did have work to do."

"It can wait."

A waitress came with glasses of water, eyeing the two of them.

"Where were you going?" Lily asked him after she left.

"Just following up on a possible lead."

"About Mark Walsh?"

He never discussed his investigations with anyone not directly involved. While he didn't want to make her wary by being too secretive, Lily didn't need to know any details.

"Possibly," he said.

"Can't talk about it, huh?"

"Not yet."

She sat back and observed him, no longer fiddling. He didn't try to hide the smoldering effect the sweetness of her attention had on him, especially when she relaxed like she did now. He sat back like her and treated her to the same appreciation.

"You're beautiful like that, you know." He couldn't help telling her.

She smiled. "Like what?"

"When you let your guard down."

"My guard is down?"

"You know it is."

Her eyes lowered, a hint of coyness, and then lifted to meet his again. "I think it's sweet that you came in here in the middle of a busy workday."

"And yet, you won't go out with me."

A breath of a laugh escaped her, soft and brief. "If you keep this up, you just might get your way."

That appealed to him immensely. He wanted to ask her if she liked being chased, but thought better of it. No, she would not like being chased. That wasn't what this was all about. She needed time. And she needed him to take things slow.

"Thanks for letting me know," he said.

He watched her study him and felt her curiosity build, as if his patient pursuit of her was beginning to open a closed door. He liked that. He liked that a lot. Once she opened herself to him completely, he'd be one happy man. Winning her trust would be one of the most gratifying things he'd ever achieved. Only with Lily, he couldn't really call it an achievement. *Gift* was a better word. Her gift to him. He wanted that so much, for her to want to give him that.

"Have you ever been married?" she finally asked.

And the question jarred him. He hadn't expected her to ask him that yet. Was she ready for this? The dating questions.

He was making progress. "No."

"Why not?"

"I haven't found the right woman yet." Maybe he was picky. Maybe he just worked too much. But one thing was for sure. He wanted to get it right the first time.

"How many relationships have you been in?"

"I don't know."

"You don't?"

He hadn't thought about it. "What do you mean 'relationships?'" He could understand her need to interview him, and he wanted to do well.

"Anything that went beyond a few dates."

"I've had a lot of those. Most lasted three months."

"You've never had a longer relationship?"

"Yes, I have. I was with a woman for four years in my early

twenties, and then I was with another woman for two years. That ended a little over a year ago."

Leaning forward again, she fiddled with the salt and pepper containers, uncomfortable again. He didn't like that.

"Are you afraid of commitment?" she asked.

"Only when I think I'm in danger of committing to the wrong woman."

"And who would that be?"

Was she worried he might consider her one of the wrong ones? If not now, then down the road? No one knew for sure what would happen as a relationship grew. "I think you know when you know."

"But what are you looking for? What was it about those other women that didn't work for you?"

"My first relationship ended because we were just too young to know what we wanted. The other…" He wished he hadn't brought this one up. It wasn't something she wanted to hear, he was sure.

"What?"

"It just didn't work out."

"Why not?" She smiled as his hesitation went on for too long. "Were you too different?"

"No. We got along. At first anyway."

"Then what was it?"

He picked up his water and sipped, taking in her playful expression.

"Sex?" she asked.

Now he wanted to squirm in his seat. When was the last time a woman made him feel like that? When was the last time anyone had made him feel like this? Cornered. Uncomfortable. Second-guessing himself. Maybe it was her history. He didn't want to offend her.

"It must have been sex."

He put his water down. "Do we have to talk about this?"

She laughed and he imagined part of the old Lily was resurfacing. That was encouraging. He didn't want her to be uneasy with sex because of her experience, so the fact that she could talk this way was a positive sign. But he wanted to be careful.

"It must have been good because you stayed for two years."

"It was good until it stopped," he confessed.

"Stopped, as in…you went days without it? Weeks?"

"Days I could handle. It was months."

"That is a long time. But you stayed."

"For a while."

She contemplated him as if she were studying a diagram in a page from a textbook. "How important is sex to you?"

The waitress appeared next to their table again, her eyes shifting back and forth between them again. She put their food down. "Can I get you two anything else?"

"No thanks," Lily said.

Wes shook his head.

When the waitress left, Lily looked expectantly at him.

So, he wasn't going to get out of answering her question. He kept his voice down. "As important as it is to anyone. She lost interest and I wasn't connecting with her anymore. It doesn't take a genius to figure that out. She just didn't have the courage to be the one to do something about it."

Lily nodded her understanding. "Sex is overrated."

Fighting the instinct to talk about her past, he chose his words carefully. "Not if you're with the right person."

Her gaze met his and darted somewhere across the café.

"I take it you haven't found that yet," he said. He didn't think he was pushing boundaries since she'd been the one to broach this personal, intimate topic. Besides, a little pushing just might be what she needed.

"I've never been married if that's what you're asking."

"Afraid of commitment?" He softened that with a grin. Let her know he was teasing.

She smiled back. "No."

"How many relationships have you had since you left Honey Creek?"

"Not very many. Three short-term ones and a few dates. I have May…"

He knew better than to press her about never being married by forty. He already knew why anyway. "Why didn't they work out?"

"The guys ended up leaving."

Because of sex? She'd already hinted she hadn't had great sex. Anybody who said things like "sex is overrated" couldn't have experienced it the way they should.

She began to seem uncomfortable so he didn't say anything about that. He was curious about one thing, though.

"What about before you left Honey Creek?"

"What about it?"

There was that sassy defense mechanism that always surfaced when she faced down her past and all the rumors.

"I don't mean to pry—" even though she had with him "—but you seem so different now. I can't help wondering…" He let the rest hang. She knew darn well what he was asking.

"What?" she challenged him. "You want to know if I had good sex? Well, all right. I'll tell you. Yes, I had fantastic sex. I loved it back then. Couldn't get enough of it. Satisfied?"

Was she telling the truth? "I'm sorry." And he was. "I didn't mean to upset you."

"You didn't." Her tone dripped with derision.

He just lifted his brow, the only sign he'd give that he knew she was upset.

She turned away. "I'm not that girl anymore."

"I know. You're someone much more mature and interesting."

When she faced him again, he saw that she'd mellowed some.

"And I'd be lucky to be the one to make you love it again."

"I don't want to love it like that again."

"It would have more meaning now." Because it would just be with one man instead of several. But he knew better than to voice that fact.

Her defensiveness slipped away with the return of her flirtation. "You seem awfully sure about that."

"Like I said, I'd be lucky."

She contemplated him, as though wondering if he'd say that if he knew what he was up against. Maybe she also wondered if it was even possible to enjoy sex again. He'd give it his best. He dreamed of the things they'd do together.

But first things first. He hadn't even convinced her to have dinner with him yet.

The warm humming sensation that hadn't abated since leaving Wes at the café energized Lily's stride as she entered the library. She supposed that conversation was her fault since she'd been the one to bring up sex. But she'd genuinely wanted to know about him. The way a man answered questions like that said a lot about his character. Wes had passed that test... except for the part about not getting enough of it. Could she even keep up with him? His drive might be different than hers.

Why was she thinking like this?

She passed the checkout counter and went into her office, going to the window.

I take it you haven't found that yet.

She'd known he wasn't asking about her marital history when he'd said that. What if he was right?

The idea of having a normal sex life scared her. But talking to Wes made her wish for it.

"You're settling in just fine, it would appear."

Lily turned and saw Mary Walsh standing there, red hair and pretty amber eyes shining.

"The library looks great," Mary said.

"Everything's running smoothly. No problems with personnel, either."

"Yeah. You have some good ones here."

Lily knew Mary hadn't stopped by to check in on her for this reason, but she played along. "How's Jake's new security business going?"

"Started out slow, but things are beginning to pick up. Damien's release has helped."

Lily smiled at the sarcasm she heard in her friend's tone. But at the same time it reminded her that Brandon was going to be released soon.

"Maybe I should give him a call," she said absently.

"Are you afraid of Damien, too?"

"No." Too late she realized her blunder. "It's just…with all the talk…"

"Yeah. That's why I wanted to stop by. You holding up all right?"

"Yes. A little gossip never hurt anyone." Well, not physically anyway.

"A little gossip, huh? Is it true you've been seeing Wes? I never make a habit of trusting what this town goes ape over."

"I wouldn't say I'm *seeing* him."

"Do you want to?"

"I'm not sure. He's seven years younger than me." And she was dealing with so much right now.

"He's not that much younger. Jake is six years older than me."

Call her old-fashioned, but it was different when the man was older. "I can handle a couple of years of difference, but seven...it seems like a lot."

"Wes is a nice man. He isn't after a twentysomething hottie. He and Jake got to be pretty good friends. I think you two would make a great couple."

"Thanks for the vote of confidence. You're probably the only one in town who thinks that." She laughed to cover the hurt that reality caused.

"No, I'm not. Bonnie Gene thinks so, too."

"Okay, so there's two of you."

Mary laughed this time. "That'll pass. You know how this town can be."

Boy, did she ever.

Emily appeared in the doorway, holding a vase of red roses. "This just came for you."

"Wow," Mary cooed.

"Delivery guy just left." Emily smiled a huge smile.

Lily was stunned. Had Wes done this? Already? He must have called right after he'd left the café. Unless he'd called before he'd gone into the café? That made more sense.

"Wow is right." She took the flowers by the vase.

She turned and placed the vase on the desk in front of her chair and sat down. There was a card. She slipped it free of its plastic holder and opened it up.

Roses are red and so are you.

Lily reread the card. What did it mean? It wasn't signed. If Wes sent these, he had a weird sense of humor.

What if it wasn't Wes?

"Lily? Are you all right?"

She looked at Mary. Who would send red roses other than Wes? Was this a practical joke? Roses cost a lot of money. Who would spend that much on a practical joke?

Maybe it wasn't a joke.

A chill accompanied the realization, running down the skin on her arms and sprouting goose bumps on her thighs.

Mary walked to the roses. "Who sent you those?" She read the card and turned to Lily.

Lily shrugged. "Someone who doesn't like me."

"You should call Wes."

She didn't want to do that. "It's probably just someone in town messing with me." Someone who didn't want her here? That was three-quarters of town. It would be next to impossible to figure out who sent them.

"It's not funny, Lily."

"I'm not laughing."

"Call Wes."

"I'll think about it." If she called him, it might give him the wrong message. She didn't want to encourage him by leading him to think she was using the flowers to get closer to him... appeal to his protective nature.

Mary angled her head in silent admonishment.

"It's a harmless prank."

"What if it isn't?"

Brandon wasn't due to be released yet so it couldn't have been him. He'd be the only one she'd be afraid of.

"No point in worrying unless there's really something to worry about." It wasn't as if someone had tried to kill her, like what happened to Mary and Jake.

Mary considered her a while. "Be careful, all right?"

"I will."

"I came by to see if you and Wes would like to double for dinner sometime. But first I had to make sure you were really seeing him."

"Oh. I... Wes and I aren't really dating."

"It doesn't have to be this week. Just let me know when you're ready."

She sounded so sure the date would happen.

Mary smiled. "I'd better get going."

Lily said goodbye and after Mary had left, sat behind her desk, staring at the roses.

Since there was only one florist in town, she might be able to find out who sent them. She picked up the phone and called.

"Daisys," Daisy Ray answered.

"Hi, Daisy, it's Lily from over at the library."

There was a slight hesitation. "Oh...hi, Lily. Do you like your flowers?"

Daisy sounded nervous. "They're beautiful. Except the card wasn't signed. How am I going to thank the person who got them for me?"

"Well, now, I—I don't know. You have a secret admirer it would seem." Daisy's tentative laugh spoke volumes.

"Who bought them for me?"

"I don't know who it was. They paid cash."

"You don't know who it was?"

"It was a young boy. Maybe fifteen or so. I don't know his name."

Was she telling the truth? Lily wasn't sure how much more she should press the woman. She seemed uncomfortable. Why? Did she think Lily was at it again? Back to her old ways? Carousing around town, hitting on men? And now they were sending her flowers?

Except that isn't what this was about. Lily was beginning to think this wasn't an innocent delivery. *Roses are red and so are you?* That could be construed in any number of ways. Red could be a symbol of beauty or passion, or one of death.

Lily shook that last thought off. Someone was just trying to scare her and she wasn't going to let them. The flowers were beautiful. She'd put them on her desk and forget the rest.

Wes stepped to the door of Jolene's farmhouse and rang the bell. Seconds later, the door opened.

"I've been waiting for you," she said.

"Sorry. I had a lunch meeting I couldn't miss." She didn't have to know it was with Lily. He was sure everyone would find out before the end of the day anyway.

"Come in."

He passed her in the entry and then followed her to the kitchen, where a cassette player lay. That was interesting. A cassette player in this day and age.

"I found it this morning," Jolene said.

And he had to assume she meant a tape. He leaned over and pressed the rewind button, but the cassette had already been rewound. He pressed Play.

"I was cleaning out the attic and found this in a box of old hats and gloves and scarves. Mark must have put it in there before he disappeared."

Wes looked at her. And she had just stumbled across it?

She was wringing her hands in front of her as she stared at the cassette player. Why was she so nervous?

"Hi, Mark," a feminine voice said from the player. It was grainy and a little muffled.

"Hi, Tina. Come on in," Mark Walsh answered.

"He had the cassette in a case and wrapped in a box," Jolene explained. "Probably why it's preserved so well."

"When did he record it?" Wes asked, hoping to trick her in case she knew more than she was telling, like maybe she knew about the tape and the reason Walsh had made a recording.

She shrugged. "Had to be sometime before he disappeared. That hat box has been in storage for years."

"You said it was important," Tina said.

Who was Tina?

"Sit down."

Muffled shuffling sounds garbled the recorder. Mark must have placed it close to wherever they sat. The voices were a little clearer now, too.

"I got to thinking about what you told me," Mark said.

"It has to be over, Mark. You're married."

"It's not about that. I want to help you, Tina."

"Help me?"

Wes just bet there was something he wanted in return, too. That was how Mark Walsh operated. He might have been murdered, but *nice* was not a trait he'd been known for.

More shuffling noises garbled the recording.

Tina inhaled sharply. "What is this?"

"It's a passport."

"A driver's license, too?"

"Yes. And anything else you need to get a fresh start. You no longer have to be Tina Mueller."

There was a long silence.

"What are you talking about?"

Good question. Wes couldn't wait to hear the answer to that one.

"There's something I want from you. You don't have to agree, but if you don't, you have to leave your new identity here and leave town."

"What identity? I don't need a new identity."

"Oh, yes, I think you do, Tina Mueller."

"Why do you keep saying my full name?"

"I know all about your past, my love. You know the one I'm talking about?"

Another long silence ensued. "Bastard."

Mark chuckled. "I bought you a house, too."

"You're crazy."

"And you'll let me in whenever I come over."

"What for? To be your mistress? Go to hell!" More shuffling suggested Tina had gotten to her feet.

Mark must have stopped her.

"You'll do everything I tell you. No one knows you in Honey Creek. You can make a nice life for yourself there."

"But only if I spread my legs whenever you show up and God only knows what else? No thank you."

"I discovered one of my wife's diamonds is missing."

Tina's hesitation spoke volumes. "So? Buy her another one."

"I know you took it."

"No, I didn't. I was only at your house that one time."

"Yes. And I saw you take the ring. You thought I was sleeping, but I wasn't."

Tina didn't say anything.

"What would the police say if they knew?" Mark asked.

"You don't understand. I had a good reason for taking that ring. I chose you because you have a lot of money. You wouldn't miss a ring your wife never wears. It wasn't even her wedding ring."

"How do you know she never wears it?"

"She has a hundred other ones."

"You stole from me."

"Please, Mark. I didn't do anything wrong back then, but the police won't believe that. If you really want to help me, you won't tell anyone I took that ring. It will give me the break I've been looking for."

"Is that all you wanted from me? Money?"

"I needed the ring."

"And you slept with me to get it."

"Don't take it personally. Someone like you doesn't care about a little old ring."

"That little ring is worth over a million dollars."

Again, Tina remained silent.

"Have you sold it yet?"

After another hesitation, she said, "Yes."

"Take my offer, Tina. It's the only one you'll get."

Tina sighed. Long seconds passed. "How do I know I can trust you?"

"Do what I ask and this stays our secret. Cross me, and the deal is off. It's simple."

She didn't say anything and Wes could imagine the thoughts that had gone through her head.

"You can make a good life for yourself," Mark told her again. "What I ask of you won't be too much of an imposition. You'll be free of your past and you can do whatever you want with the money from the ring. I won't stand in your way unless you refuse me. It's a generous offer. One both of us will benefit from."

Him more than her. He was essentially lining her up to be one of his minions. Sex probably would have nothing to do with it, despite what Tina thought.

"All right, what, exactly, do you have in mind?"

The recording ended.

Wes ejected the tape and turned to Jolene. "Mind if I take this?"

She shook her head. Her arms were folded and she looked small and vulnerable. What was she afraid of? Or was hearing the tape between her ex-husband and one of his lovers disturbing to her? He wondered if she was telling him the truth about how she had found the tape. What if she'd known about it all along and kept it secret?

Why would she do that?

The tape was irrefutable evidence that her husband had had a lover. Was that enough to give her motive to kill if Mark had contacted her recently? Or had he contacted the lover and given that woman the motive? If Jolene was aware of the reunion, she also knew it could shift the blame off her.

She could have done this fifteen years ago, too, so Wes was inclined to believe she'd only recently found the tape. And the lover had ample motive to kill Mark if he'd contacted her from his not-so-dead grave. He doubted she'd been the cause of Mark's disappearance, but his reappearance might have threatened her enough that she would do something drastic about it. After living for so long free of his ultimatums, his return would be a bitter pill to swallow. Especially if she had made a nice life for herself as Mark had given the opportunity to do with his offer.

"I don't know anyone named Tina," Jolene said.

"Mark helped her change her identity." He'd get all he could on Tina Mueller, hoping something would turn up to lead him to her.

"I searched his financial records for the house he talked about, but didn't find anything."

"I'll see what I can find."

"I almost feel sorry for her."

Wes thought she seemed sincere. "Why?"

"She was so close to pulling it off."

"Pulling what off?"

"When she met him she must have known he had money and decided to use him. For once he was the one being used. It must have really gotten under his skin, knowing that a woman used sex to get into his house and steal something valuable. I have to hand it to her."

"You're happy she stole your ring?"

"I don't care about the ring. He deserved a taste of his own deceitfulness."

He nodded. "Do you think he deserved to die for it?"

"No, of course not. That's not what I'm saying."

There was nothing more he wanted to ask her right now. "I'll let you now what turns up." He headed for the door.

"Wes?"

He stopped with his hand on the doorknob.

"I didn't kill him."

Right now he had nothing to prove otherwise, but he wasn't going to tell her that. Until he knew for certain who the murderer was, he wasn't going to eliminate anyone as a potential suspect.

Chapter 5

Lily glanced over at her dad. She bet she could count on one hand how many times Seamus Masterson had spoken to her since her return—the words *yes* and *no* excluded. Everybody called him Shay for short. Sometimes she felt like calling him that instead of Dad. She had called him Shay as a teenager and it had annoyed him.

He'd aged a lot since her mom had died. He didn't even look like the same man. Where once he'd been tall and big-framed, now he was still tall, but wiry and frail. As a child she'd been intimidated by him. Maybe that was why she'd rebelled to such an extreme. It had certainly played a role. His lack of acceptance of her had been the catalyst; that and her mother's prim way of allowing him to destroy her self-esteem. Or at least trying to.

Shay sat on the couch holding a newspaper, his thick glasses magnifying his blue eyes. He didn't acknowledge her when she sat in the chair next to the couch. Not even when she said

"Good morning." She might as well not be in the room. It was Saturday and she had the day off. She was hoping to spend an hour or two of family time with him. Break a little of that ten-foot block of ice separating them.

She looked around the room. It was cozy for such a staunch man. Bookshelves spanned the entire north wall behind her, and antique furniture over a red mosaic-patterned rug faced a wood-burning fireplace. Windows filled most of the east wall and reached the vaulted ceiling. A French door next to the bookshelves led to a wooden balcony. There was a den in this house with a television and stereo, but her dad liked to spend his time in here reading. Maybe that was his way of escaping his lonely existence. He might have seemed like a cold-hearted bastard growing up, but he'd loved her mother to the core of the earth.

Lily turned to look at him again. He still had his face in the newspaper.

May would be down any minute. They'd talked about going out for lunch and then shopping in Bozeman. The getaway would be good for both of them. It would get Lily's mind off Brandon's release, which would have happened yesterday, and May's off her troubles at school.

The sound of May's feet thudding on the stairs to the walkout basement preceded her voice. "Mom? Can I get a pair of hiking boots today?"

It irritated her that now her dad put the newspaper on his lap and looked up at May with a smile.

"Sure." She needed a pair of hiking boots anyway.

"Hi, Grandpa," May said.

"Mornin', pumpkin."

"I'm too old to be a pumpkin." But May laughed anyway.

"You're my pumpkin."

"Are you coming with us today?"

Her dad's smile faded and he glanced at Lily. It was brief. "You girls go on your shopping spree. I'll be here when you get home."

"You always stay home." May pouted.

"You get to be my age you'll understand."

"May's right, Dad. You do always stay home. Maybe it would do you some good to get out every once in a while."

Cold eyes found hers. "I'm happy right here."

"You could spend more time with May."

"I'll spend time with her tonight." His voice was starting to rise.

Lily decided not to push the subject in front of May. She'd been careful not to put too much emphasis on the conflict between her and Shay; May didn't need to be involved in all that. Lily wanted her daughter to have a good relationship with her grandfather. And the way Shay was responding to her was a good sign.

She stood. "You ready?" she said to her daughter.

"I'm hungry."

"Didn't you eat breakfast?"

"I had cereal."

And it had already worn off. The metabolism of a fourteen-year-old was something to marvel at. "We'll stop somewhere for an early lunch." It was already eleven anyway.

Lily grabbed her purse and keys and led her daughter to her truck.

"How come Grandpa never talks to you?" May asked when they were on their way.

Lily never knew how to answer these questions. The last time May had asked why she'd never met her grandfather before now, Lily had said she hadn't been close to him as a child. The next question had been, "What about my grandmother?"

She'd gotten past that one by telling May her grandmother had died.

"I suppose he doesn't know what to say."

"Why not? He talks to me."

"I told you, we weren't close when I was growing up."

May was silent for a few minutes. "Is it because of the way you were?"

Lily parked in front of Kelley's Cookhouse and turned the truck engine off. She looked over at her daughter. Maybe it was time to tell her all of it.

"My dad was very strict when I was growing up."

"Like you?"

Lily grunted a laugh. "No. Worse. He and your grandmother were religious but they were also..." *Narrow-minded and stiff* didn't seem like the right way to say this. "They wanted things to go their way or no way. If I didn't play by their script, I heard about it. Sometimes I was punished."

"They beat you?"

"No." Not physically. "When you're a parent you have to teach your children, not dictate to them."

"Grandpa did that?"

"He's changed, May. He's learned and grown over the years. If I'd known that sooner, I would have brought you back before now."

"What about Grandma? What was she like?"

A pang of sadness built in Lily's chest. She wished she could have had a better relationship with her mother. "She loved your grandpa. She did what he wanted."

"She treated you the same?"

"She didn't have to. She let him have control."

Lily watched her daughter think about that. "I would never do that."

May couldn't have paid her a higher compliment. "Then I did something right with you, honey." She smiled her love.

Her daughter smiled back. "Do you think Grandpa will change his mind about you?"

"I don't know. He never accepted me for who I was. I don't know if he'll ever get past that."

"What did he want from you?"

"I wish I knew. Good grades didn't matter. He didn't agree with my interests or opinions. They were different from his, you see."

"I'm glad you didn't let him control you, Mom."

God, she loved her daughter. "I didn't let him control me, but I made a mistake in the way I rebelled against him. That's why I got so mad when you ended up in the principal's office for fighting."

May rolled her eyes, but it was without annoyance. "Are we going to eat or what?" She swung open the truck door.

Lily laughed and got out with her. That's when she saw Maisie Colton walking down the street toward them. She was still beautiful at forty. Tall and slender with long, brown hair, she moved like a movie star. No one would ever guess she had a crazy streak by looking at her.

"Lily Masterson? Is that you?"

Maisie knew damn well it was. Lily stopped in front of the entrance to Kelley's Cookhouse, her daughter beside her.

"Hello, Maisie."

Maisie turned to May. "And who is this?"

"My daughter, May." Nothing like stating the obvious.

"Hello, May." Then to Lily, "I didn't know you had a daughter."

Lily smiled because that wasn't true. Maisie knew well and good she had a daughter. She probably also knew her age and speculated, just like many others, that May was one of Mark Walsh's children, scattered in a wide radius from Honey Creek County.

Maisie ignored her silent look and turned to May. "She's

so adorable. And she looks so much like you." Then to Lily, "How old is she?"

"I'm fourteen," May said.

Maisie's eyes told Lily all she needed to know. With all the theatrics of a movie star, her eyebrow lifted as she looked at May and then her condescension slid to Lily. She thought Mark Walsh was Lily's father.

Lily didn't even try to correct her.

"You left town in such a hurry, I never had a chance to say goodbye," Maisie said, and Lily sensed May looking up at her.

"I had an opportunity to attend Drexel University in Sacramento," Lily said. The opportunity had come much later—after she'd been in Sacramento for a while. But Maisie didn't need to know that.

That seemed to give Maisie pause. Honey Creek's bad girl had cleaned up her act enough to go to college.

"And now you're a librarian." She said the word *librarian* as if it were beneath her standards.

"She's *head* librarian," May cut in, all sass and attitude. It was so sweet to be defended by her daughter.

"Yes, so I've heard," Maisie said, scrutinizing Lily. "I also heard you and Wes are getting to be quite the item."

She'd known this would come sooner or later, the not-so-subtle queries that would feed the constantly churning gossip mill. "Really? I haven't heard that."

"How did you meet him?"

"I ran into him outside town." Lily couldn't stop her smile. If it hadn't been for her purpose for being at the prison, this would be funny.

"Wes told me you got into an accident with him, but he wouldn't elaborate."

"I wasn't paying attention."

"It's so peculiar…you two are being so secretive. Why? Where did the accident happen?"

"It's none of your business," May sneered.

"May," Lily admonished, even though she inwardly cheered. Ahhh, the candor of adolescence.

May looked up at her with all the fiery spirit of a hormonal teenager. "Tell her to back off, Mom."

"Don't be silly," Maisie said. "I was only trying to make conversation. You should try it sometime."

May squinted her eyes, making it abundantly clear that she didn't buy it, nor did she like Maisie.

Maisie grunted haughtily before turning back to Lily. "Wes must have been on his way back from the prison to see Damien when you met him. He rarely leaves town for any other reason. I still get so upset about that. Damien and all. But isn't it just wonderful that he'll be released?"

"Yes. Wes is happy about that, too." She could have bitten her tongue for letting that slip.

"You must be getting close to him."

Lily didn't respond.

"Who'd have thought…you and Wes."

Taking May's hand, Lily squeezed, a silent message to stay quiet.

"Mom?"

"We'd better get going," Lily said to Maisie. "We have plans after lunch. Good seeing you again, Maisie." It was a total lie, but she refused to let anyone take her down.

"You, too, Lily."

"Stop letting these old hags drag you through the mud!" May hissed as they headed for the door of Kelley's Cookhouse.

"Maisie is my age, May."

"Maisie who? Who is she?"

"Maisie Colton."

May's mouth dropped open and she gaped at her. "She's related to the sheriff?"

"She's his sister."

"Oh, my God. You should tell him to get lost. Is he like her?"

"No, May, Wes is a very nice man." With no agenda to slander her. At least, not so far.

Wes sat behind his desk reading a background file on Tina Mueller. Born and raised in Atlanta, Georgia, she was the only child of a plumber and a waitress. She hadn't graduated from high school and Wes couldn't find anything else on her after that. She had a couple of juvenile offenses that suggested her upbringing hadn't been stable.

His desk phone rang.

"Sheriff Colton."

"Sheriff, this is Nina Barker from Fulton County Juvenile Court in Atlanta. You called a couple of days ago?"

"Yes. Thank you for calling me back."

"I found the file you were looking for, but there's a note with a contact and a request to route all inquiries to a detective Grant Isaac." The woman gave a number to him. "This note is pretty old, though. He might not even be around anymore."

"I'll try to get a hold of him. Thanks."

He disconnected the call and entered the new number. His gut told him this was going to lead to something. After two rings, someone answered.

"Detective Isaac."

Luck was going his way today. "Sheriff Wes Colton from Honey Creek County in Montana."

"Afternoon, Sheriff. You're a long way from Atlanta. What can I do for you?"

"I got your name from Nina Barker over at juvenile court. I'm conducting a background check on someone you were investigating more than fifteen years ago. Do you have a few minutes to talk?"

"Who is it you're investigating?"

"Tina Mueller."

The detective's hesitation said he might be recovering from an unexpected surprise. "Tina Mueller, huh? That case has been cold for so long I thought it'd never see the light of day again. How do you know her?"

Wes explained about the Walsh murder and the tape Jolene had given him.

"And you think the Mueller woman may have killed him?"

"That's what I'm trying to find out."

"Do you know if she's still in Honey Creek?"

"No, not yet."

"Do you know what name she's using now?" the detective asked.

"No. Detective, why did you say her case was cold? Which juvenile offense is still open?" As far as he could tell both counts were closed. She'd done all that had been required of her.

"I wasn't investigating her juvenile cases. She was eighteen when her stepfather was murdered."

Wes nearly choked on his own saliva. "Murdered?"

"Yep. Ed Mueller was the stepfather's name. He was stabbed fourteen times while the mother was out with her weekly cards group."

Wes's mind filled with too many unanswered questions. He didn't know which one to ask first.

"You must not have received a full report," the detective said.

"I guess not. You think she did it?" And did he know why? But he'd save that for later.

"It hasn't gone to court yet, but a couple of years ago we

did some advanced DNA testing on some preserved evidence. Should prove her guilt if we ever get a chance to test for a match."

Wes started writing notes. "What was the mother's name?"

"Janet Mueller. There was a long history of abuse in the family. There are hospital reports on both the mother and the daughter. One day Tina must have had enough and waited until her mother left to use a butcher knife to stab her stepfather while he slept on the couch. He drank a lot so he must have passed out first."

"What kind of evidence do you have?"

"Prints on the knife that turned up in a Dumpster not far from their house. Blood. He must have gone a few rounds with her before he was killed. His knuckles were bloody and it wasn't his. I doubt she could have overpowered him if he fought her before she stabbed him, so my guess is she waited until after he passed out."

"So when she found out you recovered the murder weapon, she panicked and ran," Wes said.

"Yep. On one hand, I can hardly blame her. On the other, she should have gone to the police. Done things the right way."

Wes had to agree. "Where's the mother now?"

"Still living in Atlanta last time I checked."

"Do you know if she's been in touch with her daughter?"

"I doubt it. When I questioned her, she was more upset about her husband's death than the well-being of Tina."

"What about now? When's the last time you spoke with her?"

"Oh. It's been, what…something like five years now."

"You have a phone number?"

The detective gave it to him and he jotted it down with the rest of his notes.

"Will you let me know if you find her?" the detective asked.

"Yes, I will."

"Thanks for calling, Sheriff."

Wes hung up and sat back in his chair. When his mind settled, he looked up and saw his deputy standing in the doorway.

"I knocked," Ryan said.

"Come in."

"Sorry to bother you, but I think you'll want to hear what I have to say."

More gossip. What now? "All right."

Ryan didn't sit down. He stood just inside Wes's office. "My wife met up with her friends from that quilting group again last night. One of the women there said she talked to Maisie, who I guess ran into Lily on Saturday."

Wes put his elbow on the arm of his chair and rested his chin between his thumb and index finger, trying not to get annoyed. Why wouldn't those women leave Lily alone? And Maisie. Why did she have to go and stir up trouble all the time?

"She said Lily got in a wreck with you the same day you went on one of your visits to Montana State Prison."

Wes dropped his hand and straightened in his seat. Damn Maisie. He'd have to be careful what he told her from now on.

"They're hyping up the connection to the prison," Ryan continued. "One of the ladies went so far as to say you probably met Lily there. It's causing quite a commotion."

What did they think? That he broke Lily out of jail? This was getting ridiculous.

But what would it do to Lily if word got out that she'd gone to her rapist's parole hearing? So far it didn't seem that anyone knew she'd actually gone there, but how long before that changed? This kind of talk might not be good for her. As long as no one talked, it would be hard to prove Lily had been at the prison, much less that she'd gone to a parole hearing. But he'd warn Lily anyway.

"That's the same day you met Lily, right?" Ryan asked.

"Yes."

"Did you meet her at the prison?"

Wes stood up. "Thanks for telling me." He wasn't going to give away any more than he needed to.

"Sure thing." Ryan looked disappointed.

Moving around his desk, Wes stopped before Ryan. "I need you to check on something for me."

"Okay," Ryan said. "What is it?"

"See if you can get the names of every woman who moved to Honey Creek in 1995."

"Any particular type of woman you're looking for?"

"Not sure. Get me every name and I'll go from there."

"Will do."

Wes headed for the door.

"Where you going?" Ryan asked.

He paused and looked back. "The library." He grinned over his shoulder. He was going to stop by and see Lily today anyway. Ryan had just given him an excuse.

Ryan shook his head and didn't return Wes's grin.

Outside the building, Wes climbed into his SUV. He drove the short distance to the library and parked in front. Inside the building, he looked around for Lily, but didn't see her. Was she even working today?

Her assistant sat behind the main counter and saw him approach.

"Is Lily here?" he asked.

"Yes. She's in her office."

He looked where the girl had glanced and thanked her before heading for the hallway.

"I should probably tell her you're here," the assistant called after him.

He ignored her. In the open doorway of Lily's office, he stopped. She looked up, dark hair thick and silky around her face, blue eyes growing big when she caught sight of him. She got more beautiful to him every time he saw her.

"Wes?"

"Hello, Lily." He noticed a bouquet of roses on her desk.

"What brings you here?" she asked, that soft smile of hers emerging. She stood and came around her desk to stand closer to him.

"I was in the neighborhood."

That made her laugh a little. "Sure you were."

He grinned. "Would you like to go for some coffee?"

"I can't. I don't have time today."

"That's what you always say." It wasn't, but he wondered if she was avoiding him.

"No, really, today I'm pretty busy."

"Then you'd go otherwise?"

Her head angled and her eyes sparkled coyly. She didn't answer. He bet he could have talked her into going with him if she wasn't so busy. That pleased him.

Looking pointedly at the bouquet of roses, he returned his gaze to her and struggled with an attack of jealousy.

"It seems I have an admirer," she said.

She went to the flowers and pulled the card from a plastic holder, handing it to him.

He took it and read the cryptic line, looking at her when he finished. "Who sent you this?"

"It wasn't signed and the florist didn't know who'd bought them."

He didn't like it that someone had shown such animosity toward her. It had to have been someone in town; Brandon Gates wasn't released from prison yet.

"Mind if I keep this?" he asked Lily.

"No."

He tucked it into his shirt pocket.

"What would you have done if the roses were from a male admirer?" she asked.

He heard her teasing tone. Wasn't she worried about who sent her the flowers?

"I'd have bought you lilies."

And he was rewarded with a warm, flirtatious smile. He'd definitely have to get her some lilies.

"I heard you ran into Maisie Saturday," he said.

That cooled her mood a bit. "Yes. I know she's your sister, but…"

"No need to apologize. I'm a little annoyed with her right now myself." Or maybe he was being overly protective of Lily.

"Why's that?"

"She knew I went to the prison the day I met you, and now she's got the town wondering if that's where our accident occurred."

She met his gaze and a silent question floated between them. He wasn't going to say that he already knew the real reason she'd gone to the prison that day. She wasn't ready for that. But he could see how the prospect of the entire town knowing bothered her.

Wandering to the window behind her desk, she looked through it and didn't say anything.

He waited a few beats, but when she didn't move, he went to stand behind her. She looked up and over her shoulder at him when he touched her arm.

"If I could stop the gossip, I would," he said, and he meant it.

When she turned to face him, he saw how his declaration

had eased some of her tension. Moving closer, she touched his face with her hand. "I believe you."

His cell phone rang.

Really bad timing.

"Colton."

"Sheriff."

It was Ryan.

"The court order came through."

Excitement and satisfaction coursed through him. Damien was coming home.

Chapter 6

On her first day back after suspension, May saw Levi leave school ahead of her and tried to ignore her disappointment. Had he even noticed she was back? He probably already forgot about her. Why did she even care about a jock like him anyway? She didn't want him to like her, did she? He wouldn't. He wouldn't want to risk his reputation. Hanging out with her might ruin any chance he had of becoming class president.

She left the building and stepped out into a clear afternoon.

"You doing anything today?"

Peri Carter jogged to catch up to her and then walked beside her. Peri had been hanging around her more and more lately. She wasn't very popular in school, either. Everybody teased her about her curly red hair. It was really thick. And really red. Her eyelashes were red, too, and her pale green eyes were almost creepy. But she was smart and nice and didn't talk about May's mother.

Her dad was a doctor in Bozeman. Gynecologist. The boys liked to give her a hard time over that one. It was so stupid. Boys were stupid.

"Going home," May said, looking around for Levi again.

"You want to take our bikes and get ice cream?"

May spotted him leaning against a tree, looking right at her. Her heart jumped and she lost a little breath. He was so cute.

Why was he over there? Was he waiting for her? She tried to stop her excitement.

"Maybe. Let me go home and ask my mom," she hedged. What she really wanted to do was be with Levi.

"You rode your bike to school today, right?"

"Yeah, but I have to ask her." Why was she doing this? What if Levi wasn't waiting for her?

"Don't you have a cell phone?"

"I forgot it today." She had, so it wasn't a lie.

"Okay. Well, call me when you get home."

May smiled. "Okay."

Peri jogged toward a waiting line of buses and May stopped walking and looked over at Levi.

He pushed off the tree and started toward her. Her heart hammered faster in her chest. He was coming over to her. *Her!*

Wearing a white T-shirt and holey jeans, he made her want to drool. Then she realized what she was doing. She'd be dumb to trust him. What if this was some kind of joke? What if he and Sherilynn were having a good laugh over the way he was starting to make her think he liked her?

"Hey, May."

She loved his voice. "Hey."

"You going home?"

"Yeah."

"I'll walk with you."

"I rode my bike."

"Then I'll push it for you."

To heck with it. She'd see what he was all about and then worry about the rest later.

"Okay."

She walked beside him to the bike racks and found hers. He pulled it free after she unlocked the chain, and they headed down the street.

"I heard about what Sherilynn and her friend did," he said.

"Oh, that. It was nothing." Yeah, right.

"I'm sorry about that. For some reason she thinks we're still going out."

"You aren't?"

"No. I broke up with her a couple of weeks ago."

"Oh." She tried to sound like it was no big deal.

"Has she bugged you since then?"

"Nope. And she better not."

"She thinks she's tough but she's not. I'll say something to her so she doesn't do it again."

"Thanks."

A boy rode past them and looked back, staring. Levi walking her home would be all over school tomorrow. She held back a big smile.

"You want to catch a movie sometime?"

Was he asking her out on a date? What would her mom say? Would she let her? Then another thought deflated her excitement.

Was he just trying to get into her pants?

"Only if you want," he said.

"I'll ask my mom."

He stopped and she realized they were in front of her house. Her mom was still at work.

"I'll see you at school tomorrow," he said.

"Okay." She smiled and took the bike from him when he leaned it toward her. "Thanks for walking me home."

"I'll walk you home tomorrow, too." He grinned and she loved it.

"Okay."

Lily was bone-tired after closing the library. Early-September evenings in Honey Creek cooled with the approach of winter and tonight was no exception. She walked to her truck. A Ford Expedition parked across the street made her stop. She squinted her eyes to see better. She couldn't tell what color it was, but there was a man sitting in the driver's seat. It had to be Wes.

She crossed the street, feeling little sparks of excitement igniting the closer she got. Now she could see his new SUV was dark gray with shiny chrome trim. He rolled his window down and she leaned her forearm on the frame.

"Are you stalking me?" she teased.

He grinned. "Just making sure you're all right."

"A likely excuse." But she knew he hadn't liked the note that came with the roses.

"I also wanted to see if you were hungry."

"Oh...."

"Have you eaten dinner?"

She was a terrible liar so she stuck with the truth. "No. I was going to stop at the market on the way home. May and my dad will already have eaten." And her dad, she was sure, hadn't gone out of his way to save any for her.

"We could go over to Kelley's Cookhouse."

Where everyone would see them together? "I was just there with May over the weekend."

"How about McCormick's, then?"

McCormick's was a small pub on the other end of town. It attracted some regular drinkers and served typical pub fare.

They'd be safe from the quilters there. Besides that, the entire town was abuzz over Damien's homecoming. The focus wasn't on her anymore, or at least not for a while.

"All right." Why not? It was just dinner. She wasn't going to go home with him, as she might have done all those years ago.

"Climb in. I'll drive you back here when we're finished."

She opened the door and got in. The Expedition had that new-car smell and Wes reached for the radio to turn down the music. Country.

"Why don't you wear a cowboy hat?" she asked.

"Just because I listen to country music doesn't mean I have to wear a hat."

"A Montana sheriff should wear a cowboy hat." Plus he'd look good in one.

"I was never comfortable wearing them. I don't like anything on my head. Gets in the way and makes me sweat. Besides, I'd look a little funny driving an SUV in a cowboy hat."

She laughed. "Fair enough." She didn't think it would matter what he drove, though.

It never took long to get where you were going in this town. Wes parked his SUV and she got out before he reached the passenger side, leaving her purse and taking her sweatshirt.

He opened the pub door for her. It was dim inside the long and narrow bar and a football game played on two TVs above shelves of booze. Bar stools lined one side of the establishment and small, tall tables lined the other. Four men sat at the bar and a couple and two men sat at two of the tables. She didn't recognize anyone. Before she'd left Honey Creek, she'd done most of her carousing in Bozeman.

McCormick's wasn't the kind of place that had a hostess, so Wes led her to a corner booth in the back. It was the only booth and the biggest table in the place. Some turned to look at them as they passed, but no one showed any further interest than that. For the first time since returning to Honey Creek she felt normal in public.

The bartender came to get their order. She ordered a burger and Wes ordered the same.

"Has anything else happened since you received those roses?" Wes asked.

"No." Hopefully whoever sent them had had their fun and was finished now. But she knew that wasn't why Wes was asking. He didn't think she'd confide in him at this stage of their relationship.

"Getting protective of me now?" She kept her tone light, but really she was touched that he cared so much.

"Part of my job." He grinned.

She was glad he recognized her teasing. That made it easier on her to explore him a little deeper.

"Doesn't that make this too personal for a sheriff—involving yourself with your girlfriend?"

The residual traces of his grin renewed and twinkling humor reached his eyes. "You said it. Just remember that."

This wasn't how she wanted it to go. She hadn't meant to say that. She fumbled for a response, damage control.

He chuckled. "Freudian slips don't have to count for now."

He was so good at that, easing her mind. "How is it possible that you've escaped marriage for so long?" The question came to her mind as naturally as she voiced it. "You'd think a woman would have come along and snatched you up by now."

"Are you volunteering?"

The bartender came with waters. The interruption was perfect. She used it as an out not to respond.

But when the bartender left, he said, "Just for that I'm going to spend more time at the library."

She laughed softly and was surprised that the idea didn't bother her.

Their burgers arrived and they ate in silence for a while.

"When is Damien going to be home?" she asked.

"Tomorrow. I'm going to pick him up."

"I'd say I'm relieved everyone's talking about him now, but I know it can't be easy for him. Or you for that matter." In one respect she could see why some in the town were leery about his return. Innocent or not, he'd spent fifteen years in prison. That had to harden a man.

"I never care what people say. I only care what the truth is."

He'd said as much before, and that probably helped to make him a good sheriff. "How will Damien feel about it?"

"He already knows what he's coming home to. He'll be fine. He just needs some time to adjust, just like everyone else who has a negative opinion about his incarceration."

"Fifteen years is a long time."

"He'll have his moments. But Damien is a strong man, and not everyone is against him." His expression grew more somber. "What worries me is his anger. I don't blame him for wanting justice, but I don't want him doing anything stupid."

Like resorting to violence to avenge himself? Lily knew what it was like to want that.

"Are you going to let him help you with the investigation?"

"I'm sure nothing will stop him from his own inquiries. I'll keep him updated on my progress, though. Hopefully that will be enough."

She didn't know what to say to that. She didn't know enough about the case to judge. Or about Damien for that matter.

She could tell the talk about his brother upset him. Maybe

he felt guilty for not being able to prove his innocence. Maybe he was worried about how Damien would handle his anger and bitterness. It wasn't a good situation, but she remembered the Coltons as bold and ambitious. Some of them carried that boldness a little too far, but none of them were the backing-down type.

Wes was no different, except he had a softer side, one she noticed more and more. He caught her looking at him and she wanted to turn away from that direct gaze. No shyness there. His interest was clear and building, if the heat that came into his eyes was any clue.

The way that made her feel was almost foreign. She'd forgotten what it was like to have a man look at her like that, and to enjoy it. Had she felt this way at all since the rape? Had a man ever stirred such a warm glow before? No. Even before that, she couldn't recall a time she'd felt a response this intense to someone.

The bill arrived and she let herself absorb the sight of Wes while he was distracted. But when he finished, he met her look and the heat renewed. Averting her head, she walked ahead of him to the door. Outside, his hand took hold of hers, and she let it. All the way to his SUV, he held her hand. That was it. At the side of his SUV, he held the passenger door open for her and didn't try anything as she climbed in.

He was taking it slow, being a perfect gentleman. Or was *cautious* a better word? More likely he was afraid she'd shoot him down again. Or was that what she wanted to believe? Because right now she didn't feel like telling him not to call. And that was a new one for her.

She held back a smile as he got behind the wheel and drove toward the library. All the way there she felt his presence beside her. Energy hummed. Sexual energy. It had been so long since she'd felt this way—without the usual stiffening. Relationships hadn't been easy on her after her rape. She'd had to work at them. This felt different. Easy. Natural. Should she be worried? Even their age difference didn't matter as much anymore.

Wes pulled to a stop beside her truck and she froze as she looked out the window. Someone had used spray paint to write all over her truck.

Whore covered the driver's and rear passenger doors. It was written on the hood, too. On her pretty truck.

Tears sprang to her eyes. She heard her own hitched breath.

Wes swore from the other side of the SUV. "Stay in here."

She struggled to hold back her crying, but it was too much. Why wouldn't everyone leave her alone? She was so tired of being labeled. Jezebel. Rape victim. Outcast.

Watching Wes walk around the truck, scanning the parking lot as he did, Lily wiped her cheeks. He came full circle and pulled out his phone, dialing a number then lifting the phone to his ear.

He opened the passenger door and looked at her with concern in his eyes. Concern and anger. He put his hand on her knee, a comforting gesture. She listened to him ask his deputy to come gather evidence. When he finished with that call, he made another one to arrange for a tow.

How sweet. He wasn't going to let her drive the truck anywhere, sparing her any embarrassment.

When he hung up, he put his phone away and placed his hand on the headrest behind her head. He was so close.

"I'll find whoever did this," he said.

A swell of affection rose up in her. Odd how his nearness didn't make her feel suffocated. That was usually how she felt when she was with a new man. It was a struggle to overcome anxiety over his intentions. But not with Wes.

He lifted his hand from her knee and touched her cheek.

Just when she thought he'd kiss her, headlights shone on them. Wes's deputy had arrived.

Wes moved back and waited until the deputy emerged from his car, then he walked toward him. They spoke a moment, the deputy nodding every once in a while, and then Wes returned to his SUV, going around to the driver's side.

"Ryan will take care of it. I'll drive you home."

She avoided looking at her truck as Wes started driving.

"Do you need a ride tomorrow?"

She hadn't thought about it yet. "I'll get a rental." She could walk to the car-rental company.

"You can drive my Jeep. I'll bring it by in the morning."

"Really?" He was going out of his way for her. After a brief hesitation, she decided to go along with it. "Are you going to use that as an excuse to see me?"

He kept his profile to her. "Yes." But he was grinning as he turned the SUV off Main and headed east out of town. She didn't question how he knew where she lived. Her father had lived in the same house for years.

A few minutes later he pulled to a stop in front of the house. All the windows were dark. She hadn't called May to tell her she was going to be late.

She got out of the SUV and turned in the open door to say goodbye to Wes, but he was already shutting the driver's door.

Her heart leaped into a faster rhythm. He was going to walk her to the door?

The idea was both tantalizing and frightening. It also felt a little juvenile. Had a boy ever walked her to the front door before? She couldn't recall a time when that had happened. Men had walked her to her door, but that was only when she was going to let them in. No way was she going to let Wes in, and that was what made this night so different from others in her past.

She heard him walking behind her on the sidewalk that led to the front step and porch. He took her hand when she reached the door. She faced him, as nervous as a teenager on a first date.

"I had a nice time at dinner," he said.

"So did I." And it was true. She'd enjoyed every second with him up until she saw her truck. And even that hadn't been as bad as it would have been without him.

Letting her hand go, he slid his arm around her waist and pulled her closer. His movement was nonthreatening. Slow. Gentle.

He kissed her, a soft touch that was far from invasive. And it was over as soon as it began. The sweetness of it made her fall for him even harder.

"Good night," he said.

"Mmm," she could only utter. She put her fingers on her lips as he walked to his SUV. She turned before he reached it and opened the front door. The entire exchange was clichéd, it had been so simple.

Man and woman go out on a date. Man walks woman to front door. Man kisses woman and says good-night. She wondered if that's why it worked for her. It was undemanding. Easy. There that word was again, popping into her head. Wes was easy to be with. Easy on her eyes. Easy to talk to. Easy to feel good with.

Floating into the house on those thoughts, Lily closed the door and turned. Her father was standing in the entry between the living room and the kitchen. She saw his silhouette in the dim light of the interior.

"You're home late," he said.

"I went out for dinner after work." She didn't want to talk about the truck.

"Who with?"

Did he care? "Wes Colton."

"Wes Colton." It sounded like a sneer.

She didn't respond, just put her purse down and slipped out of her shoes.

"You're shooting kind of high, aren't you?"

She straightened. "Excuse me?"

"Going after the sheriff. Don't you think that's awfully bold?"

He thought it was bold of her to want to be with a sheriff. She shoved her hurt feelings aside. "I'm not going after him. He drove me home, that's all."

"I saw you kiss him."

"He kissed me."

"You didn't seem to mind."

"Dad, it's been a lot of years since I left here."

"You haven't changed."

If he couldn't see how wrong he was by now, she wasn't going to bother arguing. She started to head toward the stairs.

"Is he the only one you're chasing around town?"

Stopping at the top of the stairs, she turned. "I'm not chasing anyone."

"Don't be breaking up any more marriages. I don't need that kind of embarrassment at my age."

"I know, Dad. It has always been about you." Talk about never changing….

"You watch your mouth in my house."

Lily sighed. What was he going to do? Kick her out? He needed her and he knew it. He had no one else, even though he wished he did.

"Why didn't you drive yourself home?" her dad asked.

"My truck…broke down. I had to have it towed."

"And you went to the sheriff for help? Or maybe you planned it that way. Maybe there's nothing wrong with your truck."

"Wes was in the parking lot when I left work."

Her dad grunted.

Lily faced him fully and folded her arms. "Why do you hate me so much?"

He didn't answer, but his smirk eased a bit.

"I think you've hated me since the day I was born."

"That isn't true."

Nothing would convince her of that. Not with the way he talked to her just now. But he had his mind made up. He had his version of her all lined out in his mind, with no second chance in sight.

"I'm sorry you don't believe me," she said, dropping her arms and turning to go to bed.

"Give me a reason to, Lily."

That stopped her. She looked back at him. "What do you think I'm doing?" He was a big reason why she'd come back to Honey Creek. She wanted his love as much as she wanted the demons of her past to stay in the past.

She watched her question register on his face. He knew what she meant. And yet, he didn't acknowledge her.

Leaving him standing there, she tried not to let the crushing heartbreak of their damaged relationship ruin the enchantment of her evening with Wes. But her father thought she was shooting too high. What if he was right?

Chapter 7

In the early afternoon of the next day, Wes waited in front of the prison for his brother to emerge. Damien was five minutes late. Getting out of the SUV, Wes walked around to the other side of the vehicle, stopping when he spotted Damien exit the prison. His longish dark brown hair was on the messy side, giving him a hard look even from this distance. He wore the jeans and black T-shirt Wes had delivered for him. Damien smiled as he approached. It was a rare sight.

Wes put an arm around his brother for a brief hug. "I've waited a long time for this day."

Hard eyes that weren't softened by his smile met Wes's. "Thanks for never giving up on me."

The words were spoken devoid of emotion, as if prison life had drained Damien Colton. He wasn't a weak man, but he had a thirst to find Mark Walsh's real killer, to find justice and even retribution. How different would that effort be after enduring so much? How differently would Damien handle it now versus the pre-imprisoned Damien? More than once he'd expressed his disappointment in his family for not doing more, their dad in particular. Darius hadn't gone out of his way much to help Damien. Maybe he felt he couldn't. Maybe he doubted his son's innocence. But Wes had never doubted Damien. Neither had Damien's twin brother, Duke.

"You get anything more about why Walsh was going to meet that agent?" Damien asked when they were on their way.

"No." The reply landed like a dry thud inside the SUV.

Damien glanced over at him and Wes felt his cynicism. "You have nothing to go on?"

"Jolene gave me a tape Walsh recorded shortly before he died. One of his lovers stole some jewelry from his wife and he caught her. She admitted to it in the recording."

"And Jolene waits fifteen years to hand it over?"

"She says she only recently found it among stored items in her attic."

"Do you believe her?"

"I think she's afraid of becoming a suspect in the murder. A blackmailed lover has plenty of motive. Turning over the tape shifts the suspicion to the lover."

"He blackmailed her?"

"He never said on the tape, but my guess is he recorded her admitting to the robbery for insurance. Maybe to make sure she did what he wanted. You know, use her in some way with his business dealings, on a personal level. Something like that."

"Who's the lover?"

"Her name is Tina Mueller, but she changed her identity after she met Walsh. At least I think she did. The tape suggests Walsh offered to help her and she agreed. I won't know until I have something solid, though."

"Can I hear the tape?"

"Sure. As long as you keep it to yourself."

"I want Walsh's murderer just as much as you do."

More so. For Damien, it was very personal. It was still personal for Wes, but he also had a job to do.

He went on to tell Damien about his talk with the Atlanta detective, particularly about the murder Tina had allegedly committed there.

"How do you think she ties into Walsh's murder?"

"I don't know if she does. But think about it. Tina's stepfather abused her. If she killed him she did it to get away from him. If Walsh came back to Honey Creek after fifteen years being gone and she had been successful in starting a new life, she wouldn't be happy to see him. What if he contacted her? Suddenly her new lifestyle is threatened."

Damien nodded. "Yeah, she may have murdered him now, but we still don't know who let me take the fall fifteen years ago."

Hearing the anger in Damien's tone, Wes stayed silent.

"If he wasn't murdered back then, why didn't the evidence show something?" Damien asked, frustration coming out in his tone. "You'd think something would have come up to cast doubt during my trial. But it didn't."

"There was nothing fair about your trial."

"You can say that again. Somebody set me up."

"And we're going to find out who."

Wes wouldn't stop until he had all the answers. With the new FBI agent's help, he'd get to the bottom of it. This time they had Walsh's body—his real body, not a heaping pile of circumstantial evidence. Something was bound to break.

Wes drove into town.

"Mind if we stop at the Corner Bar?" Damien asked.

Wes glanced over at his brother. He was going to start drinking now?

Damien sent him an *oh-please* look. "I just want to taste a beer again. You'd want to celebrate a little, too, after spending the prime of your life behind bars."

Unable to argue that, Wes parked down the street from the bar.

As they walked down the sidewalk, cars passed by and there were a few people out and about. Some looked more than once when they saw who was with Wes. He noticed how Damien didn't miss it, either, and couldn't tell how it affected him.

His release had caused quite a stir in town. Wes couldn't imagine Damien would be happy with the less-than-thrilled reception he was about to receive.

One of Mark Walsh's sons, Peter Walsh, and the CFO who had taken over for Mark at Walsh Enterprises, Craig Warner, exited Kelley's Cookhouse just then. It was lunchtime.

Sure enough, Peter's face showed his displeasure at seeing two Coltons walking by, one of them none other than Damien, the man originally accused of killing his father.

"Afternoon," Wes said.

"Sheriff," Craig answered with a curious glance at Damien. Peter didn't say anything. Maybe after a while he'd come around. Things might be awkward at first, but Wes hoped everyone would see that Damien was a good man. The same applied to Lily.

Lily.

Just the thought of her made him want to be with her. If he didn't think he'd scare her away, he'd see her every day.

A couple came out of the hardware store and stopped short when they saw Damien.

Damien met their stares and glanced at Wes. "I can see some things never change."

The town was still a gossip mill. "Yeah."

They entered the Corner Bar and heads turned. Two patrons sat at the bar. All of the other tables were empty.

Tall and tattooed, Jake Huffman paused in the act of filling a glass with ice and nodded his welcome from behind the dark, polished-wood bar.

Wes followed Damien on a worn wooden floor through the dimly lit bar, past booths and tables. Damien chose a table and sat. Wes sat across from him just as Jake approached.

"What can I get you?" He didn't seem affected one way or the other by Damien's presence.

That seemed to ease Damien's tension from seeing Craig and Peter. He ordered a dark microbrew.

The bartender looked at Wes. "Water for me."

"Comin' right up." Jake left the table's side.

Wes leaned back in his chair. "What are you going to do now that you're out?"

"I don't know. Work at the ranch for a while. Eat a lot of different food. Sleep in my own room."

Wes chuckled. "Sounds like a good start.

The bartender dropped off the beer and water.

Damien lifted the mug and sipped. "Mmm," he murmured, then set the glass down on the table and looked across at Wes. "Simple pleasures are sure going to feel great for a while."

Wes smiled. More power to him. He hoped he went all out and enjoyed his freedom. But that made another thought come to mind. "Have you heard from Lucy Walsh since her father was murdered for real?"

"Nope."

"I wonder how she feels about that now."

"Really, all I want to do is live my life again. If the Walshes can't let go of the past, there's nothing I can do to change that."

Wes couldn't tell if his brother was hiding some buried emotion where Lucy was concerned. He'd been angered and hurt by her quick and easy belief in his guilt. Their breakup hadn't been clean. Now that she was proven wrong, what would she feel when she reflected on the past and the love they'd shared?

"That, and I want to find Walsh's real killer." His eyes grew driven and resolved. "I want that more than anything."

"Who can blame you?" He wanted that, too.

"I'm not leaving town until I can put that to bed."

Wes grew more alert. "You're planning to leave?"

"I was thinking about it. As soon as this is over, I'm not sure I ever want to see this place again. Or the people. Especially if they hold a crime I never committed over my head."

"It might just be the fact that you were in prison so long. Something like that changes a man."

"How? By turning an innocent man into a murderer?" he scoffed. "They just need something to talk about."

True, but once Damien adjusted he might not want to leave, especially since his family was here.

"Duke's looking forward to seeing you. He would have come with me but something came up at the ranch and Dad kept him."

"I'll see him when we get there. I talked to him before you came to get me. He told me about Dad." Damien shook his head. "Sometimes I just want to hit that man."

And Wes had to agree.

Lily stood from her desk at nine and started toward the door. What a long day. It was time to close the library.

Something crashed behind her. Glass shattered. With a strangled yell, she turned and saw a flaming ball hit her desk and roll onto the floor in front of her feet. She'd been sitting at the desk just seconds before that. She might have been hit in the head.

Running out into the library, she found a fire extinguisher and ran back to her office. Flames swirled over the surface of her desk, burning the papers she'd studied only moments before. More flames burned the carpet where the ball of fire had come to rest. Smoke began to fill the office. She sprayed the fire extinguisher just as the fire alarm went off and the overhead sprinkler shot on.

The fire was extinguished.

Lily heard her own breathing along with the sprinklers and felt her pulse ricocheting against her ribs and throat.

She went to the broken window and peered outside. She didn't expect to see anyone, but she did. A shadow standing behind the library. Pushing up the window, she coughed and waved the smoky air as it floated past her and out the window.

The shadow moved, taking the shape of a person running down the alley.

Lily ran from her office, jumping over the charred floor. She raced down the hall and burst through the back door. Sprinting down an alley, she skidded to a halt where it ended at a side street.

A car engine fired up. She ran toward it, trying to see the license plate. It was dark so she couldn't see much of anything. The car pulled away from the curb and sped away. It looked like a midsize car, a Buick or a Toyota. It was a dark color, too. Black or blue or green, maybe. She couldn't tell.

She stopped running, breathing hard from exertion.

The sound of sirens made her turn and head back to the library. Reaching the back door, she went inside the smoky-smelling library and made her way to the front. By the time she got there, a fire truck had arrived. Outside, she approached the first fireman she saw.

"We got a call from someone who said they saw smoke," the fireman said.

"Someone threw something flammable through the window of my office," she told him.

"Is anyone else inside?"

She shook her head. "I was just about to lock up and go home."

Another siren sounded and Lily watched Wes's SUV come to a stop behind the fire truck, parking at an angle in his haste, a thin bar of lights flashing along the top of the windshield.

"You wait here while we check inside," the fireman said.

She absently nodded and the fireman left to do his job, though he and his team would find no fire to battle. They'd ensure the building was safe and be gone before too long.

As Wes neared, she saw the worry etching his expression.

"What happened?" he demanded.

She repeated what she'd just told the fireman and he cursed.

"I ran after the person, but it was too dark to tell who it was."

"You what?"

She ignored his temper, knowing it stemmed from concern. "I couldn't see the license plate, either. And I couldn't tell what kind of car it was, only that it was midsize and dark-colored."

"You went after the person who tried to burn the library down with you in it?"

"I…" He didn't like it that she had taken it upon herself to chase her arsonist.

"You could have been hurt. Or worse."

"Someone clearly doesn't want me here. I wanted to find out who that is." She wondered if Karen Hathaway had been the one to send her flowers, but hadn't given the thought much credence since she wasn't the only one who wanted her out of Honey Creek. The same thought had crossed her mind when her truck had been vandalized.

"Oh, my God," she murmured. If Karen would go to those lengths…

"What's the matter?" Wes asked.

"I think I know who's behind all this. The flowers. The vandalism. And now this."

"Who?"

"Karen Hathaway. She…" Lily stopped short as the fireman she'd spoken with moments before reappeared. She didn't want this getting around town.

"All's clear," the fireman said. "But you're going to need some repairs."

She already knew that. The other firemen were getting back on the truck. This one said his farewells and joined them.

Lily watched them drive away.

"I want you to come with me to my house and stay there for a while," Wes said.

She turned to look at him. The idea shocked her as much as she was sure it would stir the talk around town. "What?"

"You heard me." He was adamant.

"No. No way. I can't do that."

"You'll be safe there."

"Wes…"

He stepped closer to her. "This is getting serious, Lily. The flowers were an innocent enough prank. Writing on your truck was bad, but nobody tried to hurt you. This is different."

"Wes…I…I have May, and…my dad."

"We'll pick them up. I'll wait while you all pack. Anything else you need you can get tomorrow."

She was stunned into silence. "My dad will never agree to this."

"Then I'll make arrangements for someone to take care of him."

Apart from her. As unpleasant as he'd been to live with so far, she wasn't ready to give up trying to close their rift. Someday she hoped he'd be able to see her for the person she'd become, not the one who'd left Honey Creek with a bad reputation. And he was beginning to show an interest in May. She'd noticed it the day she and May had gone shopping. Before they left, he'd been a real grandfather for a few moments. That was so important to her.

She didn't have to live with Wes long. This wouldn't last forever. So maybe it wouldn't hurt to stay with him a while. The security did appeal to her. She had to think of May, after all. It wasn't only about herself. If anything happened to her daughter she'd just die.

"Let me talk to your dad," Wes said.

She focused back on him. He'd do that for her?

"Come on," he said, and started toward the library.

Lily followed him inside. She hadn't exactly told him she'd go with him, but that didn't seem to matter. He'd made up his mind and she was following him. After he helped her close up, he led her to his SUV. He was sure taking charge. Normally, this commandeering attitude would turn her away, but coming from Wes, it felt good. Like a safe place to land.

"What were you going to tell me about Karen Hathaway?" Wes asked when they were on the way to her house.

"I saw her at the Honey-B when I met Bonnie Gene there. She came over to our table. She wasn't happy to see me."

"Why not?"

"She's married to one of the men I…had…relations with before leaving town."

"What did she say to you?"

She was glad he didn't judge her for having an affair with a married man. "Basically she told me she wanted me to leave town and threw water in my face."

He looked over at her. "She threatened you?"

"In a way, yes."

He shot her an admonishing look. "Why didn't you tell me this sooner?"

"I didn't think much of it."

"Didn't you?" He sounded incredulous. "You should have told me about that when you received the flowers."

"I—"

"How long after you saw her was it that you got the flowers?"

"I don't know. A couple of days maybe."

Wes sighed hard.

"Sorry." Maybe she should have told him. "I didn't think there was anything you could do. I didn't think there was anything anyone could do."

"I'll talk to her in the morning."

There he went again, taking charge. It was such a new experience for her. Usually she was the one in control, calling all the shots. Until now she hadn't liked to feel out of control. But for some strange reason it was different with Wes. She was afraid to think too far into the future.

Wes reached over and put his hand on her knee. She looked at him, surprised by the softening change in him.

"Don't worry. I'll take care of it," he said.

And a warm rush of something too close to love consumed her.

After thirty minutes of talking to her dad, Wes finally got him to agree to come stay over at his house—at least for one night. All the way there Shay had complained, but she'd seen the way he'd looked at her when Wes told him about the fire. He hadn't flinched when he heard about the flowers and the vandalism, but someone trying to burn the library with her in it had gotten his attention.

She followed her dad and May into Wes's house. It was a sizable white-pine-log home. The entry opened into a huge room with a rock fireplace that rose to the exposed purlin log roof. Pine steps on three sides lowered to a dark brown–carpeted seating area with sofas patterned in a rich-looking brown and deep blue fish design. A moose head hung on the rock above the fireplace. Past the living area was a dining table and chairs backed by floor-to-ceiling windows. The kitchen was open to the dining area. Stairs to the left of the entry led to an upper level, and next to those more led to a basement.

"Wow," May exclaimed. "You're loaded."

Lily elbowed her daughter, who grinned up at her and giggled.

"Shay, you'll probably be more comfortable in the bedroom down here." Wes didn't seem affected by May's comment. He pointed to their right, where an open door revealed a bedroom. "It has its own bathroom."

"It'll be nice not to navigate any stairs," Shay said.

"There are two bedrooms upstairs and one down in the basement." Wes looked from Lily to May.

"I want down," May said, which left Lily in the room too close to Wes.

She looked at him and then at her dad. Wes didn't seem to think anything of it, but her dad sort of scowled and, with a grumble, went to his main-level bedroom with his carry-on-size bag.

May headed for the stairs leading down beside the main entrance.

"There are two rooms off the rec area. One's an office. The bathroom's in between."

"Okay," May yelled as she skipped down the stairs.

Now it was just her and Wes. Lily rubbed the back of her neck.

Wes bent to lift her luggage. "Come on. I'll show you your room. It has its own bathroom, too."

Good. She could use a shower before bed. Her hair smelled like smoke.

Upstairs, from the loft, a log banister permitted a view of the lower level. Two doors led off the landing. Wes pushed open the far door and she entered before him. It didn't feel right with him in here, not in a bedroom. He put her luggage down and went back toward the door. The sudden flash of anxiety that had begun to build faded and was gone before he turned.

"Good night," he said, and her heart melted all over itself.

He was being so careful with her. As soon as the thought came she wondered why. Why was he being so careful with her?

Was it because he knew she wasn't comfortable with their age difference? Or had he picked up on something, something in the way she behaved? She had turned him down a few times. Maybe he wondered why, since she also liked him a lot. He probably saw that, too.

"Good night."

He closed the door.

Alone now, she turned in a circle. The room was neutrally decorated in tans and white, complementing the log furniture and knotty-pine armoire and dresser. There was a flat-screen TV and a computer, too.

Taking the smaller of two bags from the bed, she went to the bathroom just past the dresser and desk. After showering and slipping into her cotton, knee-length black nightie, she crawled into bed, so tired she fell asleep almost immediately.

He entered the dark room. She smelled him. He was tall and big and through the shadows she could see his head was hairy and he had fangs. Like a wolverine. He reached for her, his talonlike fingers clawing the air in front of her. She ran from the room, down a maze of hallways that stretched farther and farther. She felt lost and trapped. She heard him running behind her. Felt him, too. His evil presence.

Then he appeared in front of her. His face leered, light-colored eyes glowing. She dug her feet into the carpeted floor, but couldn't stop moving toward him. Closer and closer. Her hands came against him. Closer and closer, until his body was pressed hard against hers.

She screamed and writhed to get away, but she couldn't. She didn't know why. He wasn't holding her.

Finally, she was running outside. The dirt path illuminated by moonlight ended when she ran out of the trees. Now she ran through tall grass that hindered her escape. A cliff appeared on her left. The roar of rushing water frightened her. The water was dark. The river was wide and deep.

Rock broke away from the cliff where she ran. She slipped.

She was falling through the air. Fear tasted tinny in her mouth. She couldn't stop the fall.

She was falling. Falling. Closer to the churning water that rushed toward a raging waterfall. She didn't want to hit the water. It was dark, deep water. And if she fell over the waterfall...

She came awake with a grunt. Her stomach still plunged from the residual effects of the dream. Her heart hammered. She swallowed between gulping breaths.

No way was she getting back to sleep anytime soon.

Flinging the covers back, she dug out her robe from her suitcase and shrugged into it. Maybe some milk would help.

The floors on the upper level and stairs were carpeted, but downstairs the hard wood was cold on her feet. A light was on in the kitchen. Wes sat at the table.

She stopped short when he looked up from the papers he had strewn before him, pen in hand over a legal pad.

"Did I wake you?" he asked.

He wasn't wearing a shirt. She stared at him, unable to

form a response. The edge of the table concealed some of her view, but she could see he at least wore black fleece pants.

Shaking herself out of her trance, a little confused by the strength of his effect on her, she moved toward the kitchen. "No." In the kitchen she stopped again. "I couldn't sleep and thought I'd try to rummage up some milk."

He stood up from the table, putting the pen down, and walked past her to open an upper cabinet for a glass. He got a carton of milk out of the refrigerator and poured her some.

Lily rubbed her forehead, feeling a headache building. The dream still had her out of sorts. It made her think of Brandon. He was a free man, living life the way he pleased despite the harm he'd caused to others. It wasn't fair. She clutched the robe closed where it lay open below her throat.

"You okay?"

She looked up to see Wes holding the glass of milk for her. "Yes." She took the milk. "Thanks." Sipping, she kept her gaze low, struggling to push bad thoughts from her mind.

"Why don't we go sit where it's warm?" He gestured toward the living room.

She looked over to the sitting area and only then noticed the gas fireplace was running, the sound of a fan blowing warmth into the room subtle and soothing. It was too appealing to resist. Plus, what else would she do other than lie awake in bed?

She sat on a big chair nearest the fireplace, holding her glass. The fire held her gaze.

The dream still had her in that in-between state, still unable to separate it from the here and now. Dreams like that always reminded her of that night.

Drinking at a Bozeman bar. Meeting Brandon. He was another conquest. He was someone interesting enough to pursue. It hadn't taken much back then. As long as the man wasn't timid and seemed to be halfway ambitious both physically and professionally, she was interested. And an opportunity to go on a new adventure was always irresistible to her. Brandon had said he liked to hunt in Argentina. She'd never been to Argentina.

She'd left with him and he'd knocked her unconscious when they'd reached his car. No one had seen him do that and no one had any reason to be suspicious.

She'd woken to the beginning of a nightmare.

"You sure you're okay?"

Snapped out of her downturning thoughts, she looked over at Wes, who'd taken a seat on the sofa that faced the fireplace.

"I couldn't sleep."

"Why not?"

"I had a bad dream."

She watched him contemplate her response. "Not surprising after what happened."

At first she thought he was talking about the rape. Then she realized he meant the fire.

She looked away. She'd much rather have nightmares based on that. But this nightmare had been based on something real. Waking in that cabin, bound, cold. Frightened, not knowing where she was. And then Brandon had come into the room. He'd smiled when he saw that she was awake. And that's when the horror had begun.

Lily shut her eyes and fought the demons in her mind. She was so tired of fighting them. Again. She'd been doing so well until the parole hearing. It was so disheartening.

"It wasn't the fire," she said, weary. She didn't understand why she felt a need to reach out to someone. To Wes. She'd never felt that way before. She'd never trusted anyone enough to reveal such a dark secret about herself.

"What was it?" he asked.

She didn't look at him. "I didn't go to the prison to visit a friend." Did she really want to tell him this? *Yes,* her heart cried. She did. She needed to. She needed to get rid of it somehow. She turned her head to look at him. "I went there to testify at Brandon Gates's parole hearing. He raped me fifteen years ago."

Wes's expression didn't flinch. "I'm sorry, Lily."

"It's the reason I left Honey Creek. I couldn't face anyone after that, not when I was so…not when my reputation was so…" She couldn't finish.

"It's okay. I understand." He moved over on the couch. "Come over here and sit by me."

Both a command and an offer of support, she found she couldn't resist. She put her glass on the coffee table and stood and moved to the couch, sitting next to him. He put his arm behind her on the back of the couch. She scooted closer and let her head rest between his chest and biceps.

"I met him at a bar and when I left he knocked me out and drove me to a cabin near Trout Creek. I escaped just before dawn."

Wes reached over with his free hand and slipped it between her clenched ones on her lap. She let him, feeling him first give her hand a small squeeze before simply holding her.

"There were several other women who came forward after his arrest. He got the maximum sentence and wasn't eligible for parole until now. The parole board granted his release. The victims' officer told me he went back home to North Carolina. He's a free man."

"I'm so sorry, Lily. You shouldn't have had to go through any of that."

"It changed me," she went on. "Something like that would change anyone." Strange, how it felt good to tell someone about it. Even Bonnie Gene didn't know the details. "I came back to Honey Creek for about a month, but I couldn't stand how I was treated. The same as before, but I wasn't like that anymore. So I packed my things and drove to Bozeman. Got a part-time job and stayed until the trial was over. After that, I moved to Sacramento."

She looked up at Wes and saw unspoken questions in his eyes. He moved his hand from the back of the couch to her shoulder. She knew what he was wondering.

"I was desperate to feel normal again. I was too ashamed to tell anyone. It was bad enough having to talk about it in court. I needed some kind of relief. I thought if I went back to the way I was before I was raped that I could put it behind me and go on as if it never happened. So one night I went to a bar. It was scary at first. That's how I'd met Brandon. But facing my fears would help me heal, right?

"I made a mistake thinking I could do that by picking up a guy and sleeping with him. It backfired on me. The intimacy. I wasn't ready. It only intensified my trauma. The guy was nice, but he didn't have much going for himself. He didn't have a job. He drank too much. By the time I found out I was pregnant, he'd moved. I sent him a letter telling him about the baby, but he never responded or tried to contact me."

She stared at the fire again, sighing as contentment washed over her. It felt so good to rid herself of the burden.

"What was Gates like during the hearing?" Wes asked.

"Docile. Nothing like he was fifteen years ago. Could have been an act."

"Some sex offenders are nervous about facing their victims during their parole hearings, especially the ones who've changed. They want to get out of prison and live normal lives."

"I'd rather he stayed in prison."

"I agree, but it doesn't always work out the way you want. You have to move on."

"I never questioned I would. I did move on. And I'll do it again now that he's free."

"You've done well for yourself. And for May. It'll only be a matter of time before everyone else in town sees that."

She tilted her head up and smiled. "Thank you."

"For what?"

"For listening. For being here. Now. Tonight."

Leaning toward her, he put his fingers against her jaw and urged her to move her head closer to his. She let herself get lost in the warm desire of his amazing blue eyes. He lowered his head, bringing his mouth oh so close to hers. Hot, sweet anticipation tickled her senses. She closed her eyes to it, and felt his lips touch hers. He kissed her softly. His breath came faster and she became aware of her own breaths. She parted her lips, tentatively, uncertain but curious. He pressed firmer.

She spread her hand on his bare chest, feeling the hard muscle beneath. Need mounted to a feverish pitch and she sought more of him. She opened her mouth more and heard him suck in a breath of air before he slid his tongue into her mouth. He toyed with her, pulling a gruff sound from her. She wanted him.

Wanted him.

Enough to get naked with him.

Have sex with him.

This kind of urge hadn't overcome her since her younger days. And that thought snapped her back to full awareness.

Breaking away from the kiss, she stared up at him, as breathless as he was.

"Sorry," he murmured.

"Wes." She wasn't ready for this.

He slid his arm from behind her and stood. "Sorry."

"No…it's okay." She stood, too.

"I'm going to get back to work," he said, stepping back.

"Yeah. I think I'll go back to bed." As if she'd ever get to sleep now.

"Okay. See you in the morning."

"Okay."

As she headed for the stairs, she couldn't remember ever feeling this disconcerted with a man.

Or this desired by one.

Chapter 8

Karen Hathaway opened the front door of a baby-blue-and-white modular home in dire need of repair. She was in dire need of repair, too. She wore faded jeans that were too tight and a bright pink T-shirt that molded to her body and exposed her stomach, which hung over the rhinestone belt at her waist.

"Mrs. Hathaway?" he said.

"Yes?"

"I'm Sheriff Colton. Mind if I ask you a few questions?"

"About what?" She blew a bubble with her chewing gum, smacking the glob back into her mouth when it popped.

He cleared his throat. "You ran into Lily Masterson at the Honey-B, isn't that right?"

"I heard about you two. Is she trying to get you to come after me now?"

"Did you confront her?"

"Yes, and I threw a glass of water in her face. Did she tell you that, too?"

"I need to talk to you about some things that have happened since then. Is now a good time?"

Her eyes became slits between bags of excess skin that trembled as she chewed her gum. "What things?"

He removed his notebook from one of his pockets along with a pen. "Your husband had an affair with Lily in the past, is that right?"

"You know it is. Everybody in town knows it."

"And are you still angry about that?"

"I wasn't until I saw her in town. I don't want her here, prancing around and tempting my husband."

Her husband had looked a lot better back then than he did now. Lily wouldn't have been with him otherwise. She was an attractive woman. "Then you have good reason not to want her in town."

"You bet I do."

"Did you send her roses with a note?"

"No. Why would I do that? Send her flowers." She scoffed. "I wouldn't send her flowers."

"Her truck was also vandalized. Someone painted the word *whore* on it several times."

Wes saw in Karen what he would call smug irritation. No awkwardness or anxiety that would give away her guilt. "Are you accusing me of doing that, too?"

"I'm asking you *if* you did."

"No."

"Are you aware that the library was set on fire last night?"

"It was?"

Did he imagine how hopeful she sounded? Before coming here he'd done a background on her and discovered she'd had a juvenile record in Bozeman along with a robbery charge that had been dismissed in court. He waited for her to answer his question.

"No, I didn't know anything about that." She paused. "Is she okay?"

"Yes. The fire was put out before it did much damage, and Lily wasn't hurt."

Her expression drooped almost imperceptibly.

Wes remained focused on his purpose. "Where were you between eight and ten last night?"

"Here." Her smugness had returned.

"Alone?"

"No, I was with my husband."

"Is he here now?"

"No. He left a half hour ago."

"Is he at work?"

"He has the day off. Said he was going fishing." She didn't appear to care one way or the other.

"Thank you, Mrs. Hathaway. That's all I need for now." He put away his pad and pen.

She looked stunned by his abrupt dismissal.

"Good day." He nodded once and left the house.

Andy Hathaway was a middle-school janitor who spent his time off at the Corner Bar. Just past ten in the morning, Wes took his chance that he'd find Andy there now, not fishing.

Parking in the only space left in front, Wes glanced around at the quiet street and entered the bar. There were three men at the bar, one of them Andy.

"Sheriff," the bartender, Jake, greeted.

Wes said hello and stopped beside Andy. "Andy, will you join me at a table?"

Andy looked up, his reddened eyes startled. "What for?"

"I'd like to ask you a few questions."

The other two men at the bar looked from Wes to Andy. The bartender slowly wiped the bar surface.

"About what?"

"Come on over and I'll explain." Wes walked to a table a good distance from the bar and sat.

All four of the other men stared at him. Andy slid his drink from the bar, picking it up and carrying it with him. Dark liquid spilled as he set the glass down on the table and pulled a chair out.

"I ain't done nothin' wrong." He drained the drink and banged the glass down.

That's what everyone was saying to him. Wes kept his frustration to himself. "Mind if I ask where you were last night?"

"Why you want to know?"

"Just answer the question."

"Am I in some sort of trouble?"

Was he expecting to be? "No. I just need you to answer a few questions."

"Maybe I should get me a lawyer first."

"Do you need a lawyer?"

Andy fell silent. Then he turned his head over his shoulder. "Can I get another?" he called toward the bar.

Wes kept his expression neutral as he waited for Andy to decide what to do. The bartender delivered another drink and Andy drank half of it.

"I was home last night," Andy said.

"Where was your wife?"

"She was home, too."

"All night?"

He smirked. "Yeah. Where else would she go?"

Wes wasn't impressed with their relationship so far. "What did you do? Anything?"

"No. Watched a game on TV and went to bed."

Wes looked down at the drink on the table and then back up at Andy. "Were you drinking?"

Andy's smirk grew more sardonic. "Why you want to know that?"

"Were you?"

"Yeah. I have a few every night after work. Helps me unwind."

Wes wondered what it did in the morning. "Did you fall asleep early?"

"I was tired after working. Yeah. I fell asleep while my wife watched TV. She was next to me."

"When you fell asleep," Wes finished.

"Yeah. What about it?"

Wes wanted to ask if his manhood was threatened. "Someone tried to burn the library down with Lily Masterson in it last night."

"Yeah? What's that got to do with me?"

"Your wife threatened Lily three nights ago. Did you know that?"

"No." Andy swore. "Serves that Masterson woman right, though. Worst mistake I ever made was sleepin' with that whore. Been payin' for it ever since."

Wes took a moment to jot down some notes. Had Andy felt strong enough about that to write it all over Lily's truck?

"So, you support your wife's threat?"

"She hadn't done it, I might've." Andy took a swig of his drink. "Shouldn't have come back here, all the trouble she left behind. Damn near ruined my marriage."

Wes looked down at the near-empty drink and back up at Andy's pasty face and wondered what Karen loved about him. And what he loved about her. It amazed him to see people let their lives dwindle to empty shells without doing anything to make them better. Nothing improved without effort. And strength. It didn't appear Karen and Andy were capable of either. They settled for what they had and beat each other up for it.

"Thank you, Andy. You've been a big help." Wes stood.

"You gonna arrest my wife?" he asked.

"Not yet."

"Way I see it, Lily got what she deserved. Karen didn't hurt her. Lily should listen to her and leave town. Nobody wants her here anyway."

Without acknowledging Andy, Wes turned and left the bar.

Driving down Main Street, he saw a familiar truck in front of the sheriff's office. Damien was there. He was driving his old pickup.

Wes parked and walked into the building.

"Damien's here," Deputy King said, standing behind the counter. He looked and sounded annoyed. "He went into your office."

"I know." Wes saw Ryan approach, veering around a desk to intercept him.

"I got what you asked for," he said.

Wes took the piece of paper Ryan handed him. It was a printout of a spreadsheet with a list of names. He stopped walking to read. Each row listed a woman's name and the columns were filled with personal information. The year she had moved to Honey Creek. Her age. Her marital status. The year she'd married—if she'd married. Her address and phone number. Her profession.

There were five women.

He looked up at Ryan. "Good job."

Ryan smiled. "Damien asked me a lot of questions. I didn't tell him anything."

Meaning he hadn't told anyone about the list. Wes nodded and folded the paper, tucking it into his back pocket. "Okay."

He went to his office. Damien was sitting behind his

desk, his fingers typing away on the keyboard in front of the computer.

He looked up when Wes entered. "About time you got here." He stood and came around the desk to stand before Wes.

"Find anything good on my computer?" He was a little irritated that his brother had taken the liberty.

Damien chuckled. "Relax. I was just checking out places to live outside Honey Creek."

"You're serious about moving?"

"Very."

"How're you doing otherwise?" He didn't want to talk about Damien leaving. After so many years without him around, he preferred to have him near.

"Good. My house feels like a mansion and my refrigerator is my own private delicatessen. I have a little of everything. Mexican, Italian, American. Lots of chips and dips. Every kind of cheese you can imagine. Cookies. Brownies. Ice cream. Soda, juice, iced tea, chocolate milk. I didn't realize how much I missed variety in my food."

"Don't get fat," Wes teased.

And Damien chuckled again. "I drank beer with Duke, too. I tried a new pilsner. Sure is good to hang out with him again."

He seemed happy, and that made Wes feel good. "You come by just to tell me what you're eating and drinking?"

"No, I came by to see if you learned any more about that woman. Tina Mueller."

"Not yet. I have some people I'm going to talk to, but nothing definitive yet."

"Who're you going to talk to?"

Wes angled his head. He didn't want to get Damien into a froth unless there was something to froth over. He'd check these women out and see if any of them were worth investigating further. "Just some women who might turn out to be Tina."

"I want to help."

"Let me handle this part of it. If I find out if we have something solid to go on, I'll let you know."

"Why not tell me now what you've got?"

"I don't want to scare Tina away before I've had a chance to talk to her."

"I wouldn't do anything rash. I'd ask her questions, just like you. Or I'd just go with you. I want to be involved."

"Let me do my job, Damien. Have a little faith in me, would you?"

Damien stared at him a while and Wes could read his thoughts. There'd been times when he'd had very little faith in any of his family.

"I can't sit back and do nothing," Damien said.

Wes didn't respond. He wished he hadn't said anything about Tina Mueller. But this was Damien. He deserved to know what was going on every step of the way. However, it was too soon. Wes didn't know enough.

"Damn it, Wes."

"Put yourself in my shoes for just two seconds. What would you do?"

He watched Damien think about that. And finally he relented. His eyes grew less perturbed. "Yeah. I can understand where you're coming from, little brother. And I'd probably do the same thing, especially if I didn't know much. You're the sheriff, not me. Just promise me you'll tell me when you know something."

"I'll keep you updated. I promise."

Damien nodded and turned to leave.

"And, Damien," Wes said, catching his attention. "Tina might not have killed Mark Walsh." He had to prove that first.

Damien took a moment to digest that before he said, "Don't worry…I'll be keeping my eyes and ears open for other possibilities."

"That's the best thing you can do to help right now."

"Call me when you've talked to them." With that, Damien left the office.

Moving behind his desk, Wes pulled out the folded piece of paper and sat. He flattened the page.

Margaret Jefferies. Forty-eight. Married twenty years. Housewife. That meant she'd moved here with her husband. Three kids. One in college. Unlikely that she was Walsh's lover. The oldest child would have been about five when they moved here. Walsh hadn't provided a new identity for an entire family. Only Tina.

Audrey Damascus. Forty-five. Married ten years. Veterinary assistant. She'd have been thirty at the time of Walsh's recording. Two kids, seven and nine. She was a possibility.

Eileen Curtis. Thirty-eight. Divorced. Married seven years. Real estate agent. No kids. She was a possibility, too.

Betsy Grant. Eighty-five years old! Widowed. Retired, obviously. Wes knew her, too. Definitely not possible. Mark Walsh would not have had an affair with a seventy-year-old woman.

Amy Fordham. Forty-one. Divorced. Waitress. Married five years. One child, a ten-year-old. Another possibility. He had three women to question.

Wes would begin with the veterinary assistant. Her job required no formal training and there'd be no background check required. She could easily slip into her new life without anyone knowing.

He leaned back against his chair. He couldn't call any of the three women a suspect, but it was a good start. Hopefully, Tina hadn't left town.

Checking the time, he put the paper into a folder and filed it in his drawer. He was supposed to stop by Maisie's tonight. He'd much rather be with Lily. That kiss hadn't left his mind all day. But she hadn't wanted to go with him to Maisie's. He'd have to be content with the memory.

A Linkin Park song blared from a ton of tiny speakers spread out from an entertainment center. It was new and the sound was awesome. May was going to ask her mom why they didn't keep up with the times. She smiled up at Levi as he led her from the throng of dancing teenagers. Even the unwelcoming faces she passed didn't bother her. Some took notice of who she was with. That rocked.

Levi found a space against the wall. She stood beside him.

"I'll go get us a beer," he said.

She'd never had a beer before. Her mom didn't drink and had always told her not to.

Alone by the wall, May watched a group of kids dance. Some sat on a couch. Most moved around and talked and laughed while they drank beer.

Then she caught sight of Sherilynn. She stood beside two other girls, arms folded, face all pissy.

May stared back at her. She wasn't afraid. They weren't at school this time. There'd be no meeting with the principal.

As if reading her expression, Sherilynn turned away, saying something to one of the girls.

Levi returned, handing May a cup of keg beer. She took a sip. It was bitter, but had a flavor that wasn't unappealing.

"Do you like it?" Levi asked.

May nodded. "It's all right." She wasn't sure she'd try it again, though. Levi smiled. One of his friends interrupted the moment by stopping in front of them.

"Hey, Gavin," Levi said.

"You and Sherilynn break up?" Gavin asked, eyeing May.

"Yeah."

Gavin eyed May again.

"This is May," Levi said.

"I know. Hey, May."

May ignored him, not sure if he was another enemy or not. He still eyed her funny, checking her out, but not in a good way. He didn't like her. She could tell. Jerk. He didn't even know her.

"I heard your mom and the sheriff were gettin' it on."

May rolled her eyes. "What do you know?"

"Gavin," Levi said in a warning tone.

"My mom said Lily got in a wreck with him after one of his trips to Montana State Prison."

"Get lost," May sneered.

"Was your mom at the prison, too?"

May fumed inside. She was so sick of everybody saying bad things about her mom.

"Was she visiting somebody? A guy?" Gavin laughed. "Maybe that's why she never got hitched. She's been pining over a dude in jail." He laughed again.

"You're an asshole," Levi said, which May appreciated but it wasn't enough.

"My mom testified at a hearing there," May informed him.

She felt Levi's quick glance and saw Gavin's surprise with the lift of his brow.

"Why did she testify?" Levi asked. "What hearing?"

Because he was the one who asked, she looked up at him and contemplated telling him. Maybe knowing would change the way everybody thought of her mom. She wanted that more than anything.

"My mom was raped before I was born." She turned what she hoped was a haughty look at Gavin. "That's why she left Honey Creek. After we came back, she had to testify at her rapist's parole hearing to try to keep him from being released. She met Wes right after that, when she was leaving the parking lot."

"Whoa," Gavin exclaimed.

Levi stared at her, stunned. "That's awful, May."

"Is that who your dad is?" Gavin asked.

And May felt her face start to heat. "No," she snapped. "It happened way before I was born."

"Yeah, right. That's what your mom probably told you. Guess what comes around goes around," Gavin said, laughing, yet again.

May couldn't stand it anymore. She slapped him. His head jerked to the side a little but his smile went away.

"Asshole," she said, tossing her hair over her shoulder as she marched toward the door. Outside, she would have kept walking toward home, sure that Levi would side with his stupid friend.

But he didn't. She heard him jog up beside her.

"I'm sorry, May. Gavin's a friend but he isn't one of my best ones."

Over and over again Levi was proving to be someone unlike many at school. "Now it's going to be all over school that my mom was raped and she had it coming."

"I don't know about that. I think it'll make most people change their minds about her. See that she's changed. It's terrible what happened to her. I'm sorry, May. I really am."

May stopped and faced him. She moved closer, putting her hand on his chest. "You're a nice person, Levi."

He stepped closer, too, and now their bodies touched. Excitement and apprehension fired through her. She'd never been kissed by a boy before.

He leaned down. "I like you, May." And he kissed her. He

touched her mouth with his. It felt soft and warm and made her tingle all over.

She stared up at him when he lifted his head.

"Get in. I'll drive you home."

She caught her breath and got in his car. Still feeling that kiss, engulfed with the memory, she turned to look out the window.

A shadow caught her eye. Someone was standing in the trees in front of the house. She couldn't tell who it was. Sherilynn, probably. That stupid girl kept hovering whenever she was with Levi. Fine. Let her. May wasn't going to let her beat her down. Nobody would. She wouldn't let them.

Lily looked out the front window again. Still no lights. May had told her she was going to Peri's house and would be home by nine, but she'd called there and Peri's mother said Peri was home alone. May wasn't there.

Lily was worried sick. It was after ten.

Wes was up at his sister's house. He'd invited her, but she'd declined. The last thing she needed was to spend an evening with Maisie Colton. And she was still so out of sorts after last night.

Confiding in Wes that way, and then that kiss. She could have gone to bed with him. After she had gone to bed alone, she'd wished she had slept with him. It was long past time for her to reclaim her sexuality. She hadn't had good sex in so long, but she felt as though she could have it with Wes.

Trusting him was hard for her, though. Trust was hard for her with any man. But never had she come closer to trusting one than she was with Wes. It both frightened and excited her. What if it didn't work out with him? What if he discovered he needed someone younger, or someone with less drama to carry around?

What if it *did* work out?

That's the part that tickled her insides and made her breathless.

Car lights appeared on the dirt drive that led to Wes's log home.

Lily waited. She kept the light off in the front entry.

The car stopped and a boy got out. He opened the passenger door and May emerged from the car. The boy held her hand as they walked toward the door. There, Lily had a close-up view of them.

The boy put his hands on May's waist. May put hers on his shoulders, and slid them around his neck as the boy leaned in for a kiss.

Lily wasn't sure what to think of her fourteen-year-old daughter kissing a boy. What should she do? The boy didn't look much older than her. Maybe fifteen or sixteen. But he was old enough to get her daughter pregnant.

The kiss lasted a minute or two and then the boy said good night.

He stepped back and watched May open the front door.

Lily stayed out of sight until the door closed. May's dreamy smile vanished when she saw her.

"Mom."

"Where were you?" Lily demanded. She was mad as hell.

"At Peri's. I told you."

"You were not at Peri's. You lied to me."

"I was, too."

Lily walked to stand right in front of her daughter. "I called there."

May's mouth closed and she said nothing. What could she say? She was caught.

"I knew you wouldn't let me go out with Levi."

"Levi? Is he your boyfriend?"

She put her hands on her hips. "Mom—"

"Is he?"

Her hands dropped to her sides again. "Yes. A-at least…I think so."

"How long have you been seeing him?"

"Not long. A couple of weeks."

"Have you had sex with him?"

May's face colored. "No! Mom…!"

Good. What a relief. Lily could see her daughter was telling the truth. Thank God.

"Are you going to?"

"No! I like him, that's all."

"If you end up liking him long enough and want to have sex with him, you tell me first. I don't want you getting pregnant."

"Mom, stop it." May marched past her.

Lily stopped her at the top of the stairs, taking her by the arm. "You haven't told me where you were." She smelled the air close to May. "Have you been drinking?" Lily was appalled.

"No! What's the matter with you?"

"You smell like beer."

"I do not."

"How much did you drink tonight?" Lily demanded.

May rolled her eyes. "I just had a couple of sips of beer. It was no big deal."

"No big deal?" Lily's head spun. "First you get into a fight, now you're going to parties and drinking beer. What's next, May?"

"I'm not doing anything wrong."

"Oh, really? That's what you think?" Lily pointed her finger in front of May's face, still holding her arm. "You're fourteen years old. You lied about where you were going and you *drank alcohol*."

May let out a grunted breath.

"You're grounded."

"Mom!"

"You're grounded and you will not see that boy until I say you can. Do you hear me?"

"Mom, don't."

"No friends. No calls. You come home after school and that's it."

Just then Wes walked in the door. Lily let go of May's arm and turned. Seeing him was like a breath of fresh air, though he stole hers. May disappeared down the stairs, her angry steps loud, Lily was sure, on purpose.

"Everything all right?" Wes asked.

"Just having a teenager moment." Disconcerted by how good it was to see him, she headed for the kitchen. "You're home late." She inwardly cringed because she thought she sounded like a wife.

"Had something come up. I got a call to leave during dinner with Maisie. That didn't go over well. She accused me of using it as an excuse to go home to you."

"Did you get a chance to eat?"

"Not much."

"I'll make you something." Hearing him behind her, she poured herself a glass of milk and turned with the carton. "Want some?"

"No thanks. I'll just make myself a sandwich."

"I'll make it for you." She told herself it wasn't because she felt like his woman. She was only grateful for his hospitality.

"Thanks." A long sigh came from him as he sat at the kitchen table.

Taking out everything she needed to make him one of her favorite club sandwiches, Lily went to work. "What happened tonight?"

"Got a call from a woman who said her husband was drunk and she was worried what he'd do. By the time I got there, he had already left. I caught up to him after he left the Corner Bar. Had to arrest him on DUI charges."

"I'm sure his wife was delighted."

"She decided to let him stay the night in jail."

"Can't say I blame her."

Finished making the sandwich, she brought it over to the table and sat next to him. She wouldn't be able to sleep right away anyway. It wasn't because she'd missed him tonight and was happy to see him. It wasn't.

The warmth in his eyes made her smile.

He lifted the sandwich and took a bite. "Mmm." He chewed. "You make great sandwiches."

"You sure you don't want anything to drink?"

"Actually, a beer would be good."

But when she started to get up, he put his hand on hers. "I'll get it. You wait here."

She felt inexplicably warm and tingly while he got a beer and returned. And she couldn't stop smiling.

He grinned. "I'm glad to see you, too."

Fighting a girlish blush, Lily looked down.

When Wes's hand slid over hers again, she looked up.

"And I could do this every day," he said.

Every day. Lily felt herself fall into what she was afraid to call love.

Chapter 9

After three days living with May's attitude over being grounded, Lily was ready for a break. She entered Kelley's Cookhouse, leaving the cool chill of late September behind. Bonnie Gene was at the restaurant with her husband so Lily asked if she could spare a few minutes. Wes had called and said he was working late, and her dad had agreed to keep an eye on May.

She didn't know how she felt about the way things were progressing with Wes. She wasn't even sure she wanted anything to progress, not in the direction of love. When he'd called, it had warmed her with affection. How sweet of him to think of her. But then she'd realized him thinking of her that way had too much of a domesticated feel. She was—in effect—living with him. He'd called to tell her he'd be home late from work. He didn't have to do that.

Not only that, her dad had begun responding to questions she asked him. He always shut her out when she tried to have a conversation with him, but things were improving. Was it because of Wes? Did he see how well he treated her? Did that make a difference? If she gave in to fantasy, she'd dream of staying with Wes the rest of her life, caring for her dad and raising May. It felt right. And then it didn't. Most of the time it felt as if she were risking too much. If she allowed something to develop between them, how long before he started wanting someone younger? Would she find herself in her sixties facing life as a single woman again? She didn't want that.

No one had threatened her after the fire, and she was beginning to wonder if it was time to go home.

She entered Kelley's. People turned to look at her. She recognized a few of them. Mary and Jake Pierson were there, having dinner with Lucy Walsh. Mary saw her and something in the way she looked at her piqued Lily.

She went to the table, feeling other glances on the way. Something weird was going on. What didn't she know that they did?

Mary stood from the table. "Lily, I didn't know. I'm so sorry." She hugged her. Lily felt every muscle in her body stiffen.

Mary leaned back. "Are you doing all right?"

"Yes. How are you?" She wanted to deflect whatever had Mary concerned, having a bad feeling about it.

"I'm fine. Jake is keeping me out of trouble." She looked back at him and winked.

"That's good. No one's tried to come after you again?" Lily asked.

"No. What a relief that is." She met Lily's eyes. "Look, if you ever need to talk…"

Lily didn't like her leading inflection. "Thanks," she said abruptly. "I'm meeting Bonnie Gene today. Have you seen her?"

"No, I haven't."

"She's over there, talking to some customers." Jake pointed.

Lily saw her the same time Bonnie Gene turned and saw her. Bonnie Gene smiled and waved and then said something to the seated couple she'd been talking to. Stepping away, she indicated a booth nearby.

Lily looked at Lucy and Jake, and ended with Mary. "I'll catch up to you later."

Mary nodded, sympathy still in her eyes.

Oh, God. Lily couldn't breathe. What had happened? What rumor was passing around town now?

She saw Bonnie Gene and felt relief spare her. Her friend was like a beacon. A safe place to get away.

But as she slid onto the booth seat, she saw the same look in Bonnie Gene's eyes.

"What?" Lily asked.

"Oh, Lily. Everybody knows."

"Knows what?" But she didn't have to be told. Tears of humiliation burned her eyes.

"Gavin MacGregor told his mother. It spread from there."

"Who is Gavin MacGregor?"

"He's a junior at Honey Creek High. Levi Garrison is one of his friends. Levi and May were at the same party last weekend. Apparently they talked to Gavin."

May had talked. May told someone about what had happened to her? Her own daughter? Surely it hadn't been on purpose.

"They know you were raped. Some are saying May is your rapist's daughter. Oh, Lily, I'm so sorry. I know how upset this is going to make you."

Lily could only stare down at her hand on the table.

"I've told everyone I know that May's father isn't who they think it is."

Which was only going to make things worse. As soon as the details emerged—and they would—they'd know it hadn't been that long after her rape that she'd slept with May's father.

Lily looked around. Almost every eye in the place was trained on her. Some looked away when she caught them, others didn't. Some turned to talk with their tablemates.

A tremble began in her limbs. She wiped a traitorous tear from her cheek.

"Lily?"

She wanted to get up and walk out of here, but that would mean parading in front of everyone. She felt like a rape victim again. Helpless. What was she going to do?

She didn't know. She only knew she was lost and afraid. The front door opened and Wes walked in. Her heart overflowed with need. She needed him so much right now and he was here.

He searched the restaurant until he found her. His face was set and grim.

He knew. She needed him. He'd known, and he'd come for her.

Another tear rolled from her eye and more followed. There was no stopping them now.

Wes strode toward her, all purpose and brawn heading her way. It was the most beautiful sight in the world to her.

"Oh, my…look at him," Bonnie Gene said.

Lily's emotions overwhelmed her. He was going to rescue her. That's what it felt like. Unless she was wrong and he had another reason to be here. But she doubted that, especially when he reached the table and extended his hand.

"Come with me," he said.

She wiped her cheek again and gave him her hand.

"Bonnie Gene," he said.

"Wes. Your timing couldn't be better."

"I tried to catch you before you got here," he said to Lily.

She let him put his arm around her and escort her toward the door. He must have called home again, after learning what was going around town, and worried she was in the middle of spectator hell. She was. The restaurant was quiet as they passed, all the way to the exit.

Maybe moving here had been a mistake after all.

Wes opened the door for her and she got into his SUV. He shut the door and moved to the other side. When he sat behind the wheel, he looked over at her. After a minute, he started driving. But just outside of town he pulled off the road onto a side street and parked along the side of the dirt road.

She looked over at him, wondering why he'd stopped.

His face was intent as he hesitated. "I'm sorry this is happening, Lily, But I have to ask. Why, after fifteen years, do you still need to keep a secret?"

Bowing her head, she stared at her clasped hands in her lap. "You know why."

"It wasn't your fault."

"Yes, it was. I picked him up at a bar. I did that all the time."

"You were young."

"I should have known better. Things weren't great at home, but taking personal risks wasn't the way to fight back." She lifted her head and turned toward him. "I hurt myself more than I hurt my parents. That's what I was trying to do. Hurt them. And look what it got me."

"You have to stop blaming yourself, Lily."

"I'm over it. I am. It's just…with Brandon's release and all…it set me back, that's all."

"Yes, it set you back, but there's more to it than that. You've kept this buried too long."

"You think I shouldn't mind if the whole town is talking about me…about *that?*"

"No. I don't think anyone would like that. I think you should stop blaming yourself."

She did blame herself. She'd never thought of it that way, but now she realized she did. Sleeping around the way she had, it was hard not to hold herself accountable. But she hadn't set out to get raped. No woman deserved that, no matter how debauched her lifestyle.

Yet again, Wes had done something incredibly sweet. He cared about her. He'd rescued her. He was still rescuing her. Helping her heal. Never before had she trusted a man this much.

Removing her seat belt, she leaned over the console. His face was close to hers now.

"Don't stop holding your head high," he said.

She slid her hand along the side of his face and ran her fingers into his rich, brown hair. He didn't make a move, which only sweetened the moment more.

She pressed her lips to his. He let her have control. He responded to her kiss, but didn't push further. She parted her lips and pressed harder.

He answered her.

Soon his arms were around her and she was arching toward him. It felt so good. And safe. He was the first man in fifteen years who made her feel that way.

She broke away to unbutton his shirt. When she slid her hands over his chest and pushed the material off his shoulders, he put his hands over hers.

"Lily."

She looked up into his impassioned eyes. "I want this."

"Not here."

Yes, here. It was a rush to feel like her old self again, only this time she was in control. This time she wasn't doing anything to rebel against her parents. This was real. It meant something.

Climbing into the backseat, she sat and patted the space beside her. Wes had twisted to watch her, and now he hesitated.

His hesitation only made her want him more.

"Come here."

"Lily…"

"Please."

At last he climbed into the back, his big body not fitting between the seats as well as hers had. He sat beside her. She crawled onto him, straddling his thighs.

He put his hands on her hips.

She kissed him.

"I don't have anything," he said.

"Diseases? Good," she teased, kissing him some more.

"That's not what I meant."

She laughed because she already knew that, pushing his shirt down his arms. "It's okay." He shrugged out of his shirt, still looking uncertain. Pulling her long-sleeved white T-shirt over her head, she dropped it on the seat beside her, loving how his gaze fell.

When his eyes lifted, she unbuttoned his jeans. He didn't look so uncertain anymore.

Climbing off him, she took off her jeans and removed her underwear. The sound of his breathing was an aphrodisiac. On her knees, she waited for him to get naked. When he left his jeans and boxers on the floor, she climbed back onto his lap, positioning herself on the length of his erection, but nothing more. She needed a little more time.

Kissing him, her pulse grew heavier as his hands roamed. She tipped her head back when he put his mouth on her breasts. His hands kneaded her butt, moving her against him. The slow and steady grind against his hardness heated her. She moved with him. He groaned and found her mouth, kissing her deep.

She continued to move with his coaxing. Urgency made her ache unbearably for him.

Now she was ready.

Raising up on her knees, she reached down and put him where he needed to be, and then let her weight slowly draw him inside. He fitted her perfectly and let her keep the pace.

But she was clumsy in her movements, as if it were her first time. In a sense, it was. She'd started her life over after her ordeal. The sex partners she'd had since then had been all wrong. Stiff and unpleasant. This was the opposite. Right. Warm. Exquisitely pleasurable.

Wes held her hips and began to thrust his own upward. She put her hand on the roof to keep her head from hitting it. Tingles of ecstasy sailed through her. An orgasm grew, rapid and out of control. She shouted when it burst over her. Wes rammed his erection into her until a sound from deep in his throat told her he'd reached the same peak.

Sagging against him, she laid her head on his shoulder and basked in the wonder while her pulse slowed and her breathing came back to normal.

It had been beyond her hope ever to feel like this again. But somehow Wes had overcome that obstacle. How frightening to realize the significance. How frightening to realize the significance of him. Wes. Could he really be hers?

A long-buried part of her cried, *yes.*

Lily didn't come down from Wes's room until late the next morning. He'd already left for work. She'd barely awakened when he'd leaned over the bed and kissed her. But now the memory of that and of what had transpired after they'd come home last night had her floating inside.

Seeing her dad and May at the kitchen table, she was a

little embarrassed. If either one of them had gone upstairs, they'd know where she'd slept.

Her dad and May stopped talking when she neared.

"Don't you have to work today?" her dad asked.

He was actually talking to her? "I have the day off." Thank goodness. She couldn't have woken up early after last night. She turned to May, "Why aren't you in school?"

"I told her she could take the day," her dad said.

"What gives you the right to do that?" Lily snapped.

"I wanted to talk to you," May said.

Lily went into the kitchen and poured herself a glass of iced tea from a pitcher that Wes kept in his refrigerator. She was still upset with May and hadn't decided how to deal with it.

"Keeping things bottled up is never a good thing," her dad said. "Neither is moping in your room all day."

She turned and looked from May's somber face to her father's. May must have told him everything. "I wasn't going to stay in there all day."

"You should have told us what happened back then."

"You and Mom? What would you have done?"

"Helped you. Something."

"Really?" She couldn't subdue her animosity. "I doubt you'd have done anything but blame me." Her parents had never really been there for her. She'd never felt as if she could turn to them. And while she'd moved here to mend that relationship, the reminder that the whole town was gossiping about her rape put her in a foul mood.

Her dad looked annoyed. "You made it hard for us, Lily, with all your gallivanting. But we wanted the best for you."

"You wanted me to be someone I wasn't."

"That isn't true. We wanted you to succeed."

"Nothing I could have done would have made you think I succeeded."

Her dad sighed. "Well, that part about you hasn't changed. You're still as hardheaded now as you were then."

There it was, his disapproval. She'd known it would come up sooner or later.

"My mom isn't hardheaded," May put in.

But Shay ignored her. "If you'd done something to make us proud, we would have been," her dad said.

"Like what?"

"Get good grades. Go to college."

"I did get good grades." She'd had a B average but that hadn't been good enough.

"You had no aspirations other than going to parties and being with boys."

It would have been different if her parents had loved her for who she was. But she didn't comment on that. Instead, she sipped her tea.

"I hate to say it, Lily, but it's no wonder you were raped."

Her hand trembled and she almost dropped the glass.

"What I can't figure is how you could have gone out and done it again right after that."

Meaning how she'd gotten pregnant with May.

"I don't regret that."

"No, you have May, but…hell, Lily, have you no respect for yourself?"

"Stop it!" May yelled and then she pointed at Shay much the same as Lily did when she was mad. "You leave her alone."

Shay pushed back his chair and stood. "There's no talking to you, Lily, you never listen." With that he left the room and then the house, the front door shutting with a thud.

Lily turned toward her daughter.

"Mom, I didn't mean to start anything."

The look of heartfelt appeal on her daughter's face seared her. "I know you didn't."

"It's just that that boy kept saying bad things about you and I couldn't stand it anymore."

So she'd thought she'd defended her mother telling that boy about her mother's tragedy would make him stop thinking of her negatively.

"And your reaction backfired. When are you going to learn to stop lashing out in a difficult confrontation?"

"I'm not like you, Mom. I'm not going to sit back and let anyone slander me. Or you."

"And now everyone will look at me like I'm weak and vulnerable. I didn't want that."

"I know." She still looked pleading. "I'm sorry."

Lily moved closer and hugged her daughter. "You don't have to be sorry. I know you didn't mean any harm. I love you. The talk will pass."

The sooner the better.

Sitting in his SUV, Wes tried to concentrate on the entrance to the veterinary clinic where Audrey Damascus worked. He wanted to catch her when she left. But he kept sinking into heated memories of Lily. He couldn't stop his brain from going there. Checking his watch, he figured he had a few minutes, so he finally gave up and leaned his head back against the seat and shut his eyes.

The last thing he'd expected was that Lily would want to have sex in the back of his SUV. It resembled the old Lily, and yet it didn't. Some of her adventurous spirit had returned, but rather than a reckless impulse, growing trust in their relationship had compelled her. Wes had felt it with her, and it had drawn him closer than ever. After connecting with her like that, he was worried about what it would do to him if she ever turned away from him.

And then they'd gone home and she'd slept with him. At around three he'd awakened to find her watching him, and this time he'd taken control. She hadn't been afraid and that had arrowed straight through him. Making love with her was intense that time. He couldn't wait to do it again.

Wes opened his eyes and watched the clinic. He wished he could leave right now.

Just then, Audrey Damascus emerged. It was five-fifteen. Good. The sooner he got this over with the sooner he could go home to Lily.

He got out of his SUV and approached her as she reached her car, a dented and fading Honda Civic. He had known from her driver's license that she was a little on the heavy side, but he would never have guessed she was this overweight. If she'd been involved with Mark Walsh, she must have been a lot thinner. Or maybe Mark had secretly liked heavier women.

She stopped at her driver's door and saw him.

"Audrey Damascus?"

She eyed him in surprise.

"I'm Sheriff Colton." He showed her his identification.

She glanced down and then looked up at his face. "I know who you are."

He took out his notepad and pen. "I need to ask you a few questions. Do you mind?"

"What about?" She appeared genuinely perplexed.

"Did you know Mark Walsh?" he asked.

Her brow creased above her nose. "The guy that was murdered?"

"Yes."

"I know *of* him. It's a small town. Are you asking me if I knew him personally?"

"Yes."

A breath of a grunt accompanied the wonder in her eyes. "No, I didn't. Why are you asking me that?"

"You moved to Honey Creek in 1995, isn't that right?"

"Yes. How did you know that? Why are you checking up on me like this?"

Her voice didn't sound like that from the recording, but the tape was old. "Why did you move here?"

She hesitated as she searched his eyes for answers he could only guess were swimming in her head. "My husband has family here. We were just dating back then, but I moved here with him."

That would be easy enough to check. "What was your maiden name?"

"Murdock."

He jotted that down.

"Look, Sheriff, I've done nothing wrong, especially where Mark Walsh is concerned. I didn't even know him."

"You never met him? Not even once?"

"No."

"Do you know anyone by the name of Tina Mueller?" He watched her face for telltale signs.

She shook her head. "Never heard of her. You gonna tell me what this is all about?"

This was a waste of time. Wes knew it right then. Her bewilderment was too real to miss. She didn't know anything and she'd never been involved with Mark Walsh.

He closed the notebook. "Thanks for your cooperation."

"Wait a minute. What made you ask me about Mark Walsh?" Audrey asked as he walked toward his SUV.

He turned. "Sorry to have bothered you."

She put her hand on her hip and looked frustrated that he refused to tell her anything. It was better that way. He faced forward again and made it to his SUV. He didn't want to alert Tina Mueller that he was on to her. Hopefully he'd find her before word got around that he was asking about her.

Next on his list was Eileen Curtis and then Amy Fordham. He drove the short distance to Curtis Real Estate Agency, but didn't get out right away. It was almost six now. If he got home too late, maybe he'd wake Lily up. He wondered if she knew he wanted her to sleep in his bed from now on. If she didn't, he'd have to make sure she did. Like, now.

He pulled his phone from his pocket and called her. She answered on the second ring.

"Hi," he said when she answered.

"Wes?"

"How are you?"

"I'm fine. Just leaving work. How are you?"

"I had to hear your voice."

"Oh." She sounded tentative, as if this transition in their relationship was too new for her. "It's good to hear your voice, too."

He wanted her to mean that. But he wasn't sure if she did. Maybe she needed time to get used to this. He was okay with that. He was a patient man. "This is turning into a long day. I have to talk to some people and then I have to finish up at the office. I'll be a little late getting home. I wanted to let you know."

"All right. I'll wait up for you."

His heart soared. "That would be great." She might be a little skittish right now, but she was still attracted to him.

He could hear her breathing. They didn't say anything, but he could feel the energy between them.

"I'll see you when you get home then," she said, her voice sultry now.

"I can't wait."

"Me neither."

He was the luckiest man alive. "Bye."

"Bye," she whispered, and he could picture her smiling.

He disconnected. That was more like it. Looking toward the old house that was now a business, he steered his focus back on work.

He got out of his SUV. Eileen had done well for herself over the years. She lived in a refurbished old house in town and her real estate business had grown to service other towns in the county. He had seen Eileen around Honey Creek, but he'd never had a chance to talk to her and get to know her. She had a reputation of being friendly to everyone, Colton or Walsh, it didn't matter. Once, a long time ago, a rumor had traveled around that his dad had had an affair with her, but that turned out to be false. His mom had had a hard time with that, but things had mellowed after it was discovered Eileen had gone to Vegas the weekend they were purported to be together. Ryan had filled him in on that, compliments of his gossipy wife.

Wes stepped to the door of Eileen's real estate agency and opened it, a good sign she was still here. The living room was a seating area with a desk on one side. This room opened to what once had been the kitchen but now was a conference room. Two other doors were open, one off the conference room, the other off the living room. Through that door he heard the sound of someone tapping on a keyboard.

The tapping stopped when he shut the front door.

Eileen Curtis appeared a few seconds later. Her short hair was dyed blond, a little on the harsh side. She had green eyes. Dressed in expensive-looking brown slacks and a cream-colored turtleneck with a brown scarf around her neck, her trim body showed her healthy lifestyle.

"Good afternoon, Ms. Curtis."

"Sheriff?" she queried. "Don't tell me you're looking for a new house. I can't imagine there's a better place for you to live than your ranch."

He smiled. "I'm not here to find a new place."

"What a relief." She smiled back, straight white teeth another clue to her healthy and successful lifestyle. Her image lived up to her reputation in town.

"I need to ask you a few questions."

"Wow. Should I be flattered?"

"It's about Mark Walsh."

Her smile faded. "Oh, that. I heard he showed up dead again. I'm so sorry. Your brother…"

"Thanks. We're all really happy he's free."

"That must be so hard for him. After all these years…"

"Yes."

She swung her arm toward the conference table. "Would you like to sit down? Can I get you some water or anything?"

She wasn't flustered at all. Wes went to the table. "I don't need anything to drink, but thanks."

He sat and so did she, across from him.

"You have me at a loss," she said. "What do you think I know about Mark Walsh?"

"Did you know him?"

"Me?" She breathed a laugh. "No. It's a little hard to get to know a dead man, isn't it?"

Wes smiled at her attempted humor. "You moved here the year he was supposedly killed the first time, didn't you?"

"Was that when it was?" She lifted her head and looked upward as though searching her memory. "Yes, I think it was the same year."

"And you never met him?"

"No. What makes you think I might have?"

"I'm not sure. That's why I'm asking."

"Are you asking every woman who moved here the same year he was killed?" she asked.

"Something like that."

She considered him a moment. "I heard he had a lot of lovers. Are you questioning all the women who might have gotten involved with him?"

Why had she brought that up? She'd denied knowing or ever meeting Walsh so asking her wouldn't do him any good. If she had been involved with Walsh, and she was Tina Mueller, she'd deny it.

"Where are you from originally?" he asked instead.

She eyed him curiously before answering. "I was born in Austin, Texas. I lived there until I came here."

"What made you choose Montana?"

"I wanted to stay west, but I didn't want the heat."

"And Honey Creek?"

"Why Honey Creek?" She looked upward again. "I moved to Bozeman originally, but after checking the area out, I fell in love with this town. It gets a little trying knowing everyone who lives here and them knowing everything about you, but I love the small-town feel, and when no one is taking jabs at others, it's a supportive community."

So she didn't like her privacy invaded? "What about your family?"

"I was an only child and both my parents are dead now."

"I'm sorry."

Her soft smile said she appreciated his condolence.

"You're divorced, is that right?"

"Yes."

"Is Curtis your married name?" He knew this, but asked anyway.

"No, I kept my name when we married."

Wes nodded. "Where's he now? Your ex-husband."

"He moved to Billings."

Wes jotted that down on his notepad along with his name, which Ryan had already given him.

"Do you mind my asking what all this has to do with Mark Walsh's murder?"

"Maybe nothing. I'm just trying to gather all the information I can," he said, standing. "I think that's all I need. Thank you for your cooperation."

"Anytime, Sheriff." She stood with him and smiled.

He nodded his farewell, wondering if she was another dead end. She didn't seem to have anything to hide, but then, some liars were better than others.

Wes sat at a table in Amy Fordham's section. The hostess hadn't seemed too pleased with his request. The tables were filling up, but he wasn't going to take long. It was already after eight and he was anxious to get home to Lily.

He missed her and it hadn't even been twenty-four hours since he'd last seen her. And she had baggage he was afraid she wouldn't be able to drop. For once he found a woman he thought would fit in his life, and she had a traumatic past and issues with their age difference. He'd never had to go after a woman this hard before, but he swore he'd do it with Lily. Because one thing he was sure of…he wanted many repeats of last night.

He hoped she felt the same.

The waitress approached his table.

"Hi, I'm Amy. Can I get you something to drink to start out?"

Her voice was a little gravelly from smoking and she seemed a little rough around the edges.

"Actually, I won't be long." He showed her his badge. "Sheriff Colton. Will you have a seat for a minute?"

She glanced around at the other tables.

"This won't take long," he said, and pushed out the chair next to him.

She looked at him. "Did something happen?"

Her curly hair was clipped back and her skin had a slight sheen to it from sweating, but she was an attractive woman, in good shape and looking young for her age and smoking habit. He could imagine Walsh going for a woman like her. Big breasts and all.

"You've heard about Mark Walsh's murder?"

Her confused nod answered him.

"Please, sit down. I need to ask you a few questions."

"I didn't have anything to do with Walsh's murder."

"Where are you from?"

"Why are you asking me that? Am I a suspect or something?"

He smiled as kindly as he could. "No. Not at all. I'm just trying to piece some things together."

"And you think I can piece them together for you?" Her eyes grew dubious. "You must not have much to go on."

"Sit down, Amy." This time there was no invitation in his tone.

She sat, eyes a little more apprehensive now.

"Where are you from?" he asked.

"Bozeman."

"What brought you to Honey Creek?"

"My mom lived here. I came here after my first divorce."

He asked what her ex-husbands name was and she told him.

"What is your maiden name?"

"Why do you need to know that?" She looked from his notepad where he was busy writing to his face.

"Was it Fordham?" he asked.

"No, that was my second husband's name. We had a child together."

"What was your maiden name?"

"Smith."

Was she lying? Amy Smith? Well, he hadn't expected anyone to tell him her maiden name was Mueller.

"How long have you been divorced from your second husband?"

"Seven years."

"Is he from here?"

"He was. He moved away after our divorce."

"Where did he go?"

"Why would I care? He cheated on me. He probably moved to his lover's hometown in Boise."

He was careful not to feed on her emotions. "Did you know Mark Walsh?"

"I heard his name around town. I never met him, though."

"Why did you and your first husband divorce?" He was fishing for a connection to Walsh. If she had an affair…

"We were too young when we met. We grew apart."

"Did you have an affair with anyone?"

She laughed cynically. "You mean with Walsh? No. Guys like that don't turn me on. I like them younger than me—not the other way around. My boyfriend is three years younger than me."

He studied her for a moment. There really wasn't anything else to ask at this point. He had enough to go on for now. He could corroborate her answers with her ex-husband's, and maybe one of them would reveal something.

He stood from the table. "Thank you. That's all for now."

Her eyes followed his movements. "Why do you think I knew Walsh?"

"You've lived here long enough to have met him," he said, knowing it was noncommittal and vague. He nodded a farewell. "Thanks again." And with that, he left.

Maybe something would turn up on her, maybe something wouldn't. Eileen had been willing to cooperate, maybe too willing, and Amy had been apprehensive and had the hardened persona to go with a Tina Mueller past. Eileen was much more refined and a lot more successful. Not the makeup of a woman capable of killing a man. Or men, if she had, in fact, killed her stepfather and then Walsh.

He didn't want to think about all that anymore tonight.

All he wanted was to go home to Lily. Unfortunately, he still had things to wrap up at the office. With any luck, he'd get home by ten or a little after. Lily said she'd wait up for him. He hoped it wasn't too late when he got home.

Chapter 10

Lily took the rolling cooler from the passenger seat of the Jeep and pulled it toward the sheriff's office. Her heart beat in tune with her nerves. Maybe this impulse was too much too soon. It was his phone call. It was so sweet. She hadn't been able to get him out of her mind ever since. So she'd packed dinner for two and driven to his office where he'd said he had to finish up. She wasn't even sure he'd be here yet, but she wanted to surprise him.

Inside, the office was quiet. Tugging the cooler along, she moved around the front counter and headed for the only office with a light on.

At the entry, she stopped. Wes stood behind his desk, stuffing a folder into a narrow, soft leather briefcase. The sight of him stole over her, like an electric current of love.

He looked up and grinned. "I was just thinking about you."

The warm gush that greeting gave her nearly made her face heat up.

He glanced down and saw the cooler. "I was about to leave and come home."

Should she have waited for him? "Have you already eaten?" As busy as he was, she didn't think he had.

Moving around the desk, he shook his head. "No. I haven't had time."

God, he was sexy. She wheeled the cooler into the office, stopping in front of him.

His eyes took in her face. "There's a table in the conference room." His voice was all gravelly and made her tingle.

"Here's fine." She knelt to unzip the front compartment of the cooler. Inside, she took out a blanket and spread it on the floor, glad to have something to keep her busy.

"That's handy." He knelt down beside her and then sat, leaning against the office wall. "Guess there are some parts of the old Lily that haven't changed."

She looked over at him and was relieved to see he was teasing.

"Your adventurous part," he added. "That's all I meant."

Smiling, she unzipped the top compartment of the cooler and took out the bagged sandwiches and a container of crab salad. Next came a bag of chips.

"In case you can't tell, I don't cook much," she said.

"Looks like we'll be spending most of our money at the deli counter then."

"I can cook some things. Boiled eggs. Hamburgers. Hot dogs."

When she'd finished arranging everything, she leaned against the wall beside him. Handing him a roast beef sandwich on a paper plate, she dished him up some crab salad. Next, she took care of her own plate.

After they'd eaten for a few minutes, she asked, "Don't you get tired of working so much?"

"It isn't always like this. There's just a lot going on right now."

Meaning Mark Walsh's murder. The fire in the library...

"I feel like I'm partially to blame for that."

"Not to blame. I want you safe. It's my job."

"I feel safe with you." She smiled and loved how he noticed.

"Good. That's quite a compliment."

"Why do you say that?"

"A woman with your history? It can't be easy." He bit into his sandwich.

He meant the rape. "No, but I don't want to be treated like I'm helpless, either."

Looking at his face while he chewed and swallowed, he said, "I can tell that about you. And it's commendable."

"There are some who wouldn't agree." She took another bite of her own sandwich.

"Like who?"

She waited until after she swallowed her bite. "Like the victims' officer at the parole hearing. She was awful."

"She meant well. She cares about you."

Lily thought that was an odd thing to say. "How do you know that?"

"She told me." He put his sandwich down, abandoning another bite.

Lily froze. "What did you say?"

Slowly, he met her eyes.

A chill of foreboding chased her euphoria away. "When did you talk to her?"

He hesitated. "After I met you."

"After?" She put her sandwich down on her plate.

"Lily, don't be upset. I knew you were lying about why you were at the prison and I just wanted to know why."

"So you…you…you went behind my back? You…you checked up on me?" Without telling her? Why had he kept it from her? That stung. Disenchantment swirled inside her. And here she'd been beginning to think he had real potential.

She removed her plate from her lap and put it on the blanket, no longer hungry.

"I wanted to know why you were at the prison."

"That was none of your business."

"I made it my business. I've been interested in you since the first day I met you."

"So you wanted to…what…make sure I wasn't involved with a criminal?"

He didn't answer. "Lily, please. It was a harmless inquiry."

Harmless? Her rape was an intensely personal matter. "What did she tell you?"

"That you testified at Brandon Gates's parole hearing." He paused. "And why."

Lily's now bloodless face felt cold. "You knew. All this time, you knew."

"I…"

She felt betrayed. "Why didn't you tell me?"

"I wanted you to be ready to tell me on your own."

"And I did." She remembered how much it had meant to her, to unburden herself, to trust him enough to do so. And the whole time, he'd already known. She felt humiliated. She'd bared her soul to him and he'd already known. A lump of hurt gathered in her throat.

"How could you?" Absurdly, she felt like crying. She didn't want to be a baby about it.

He put his plate down next to hers and propped his weight

on one hand as he leaned toward her. "Lily, I was only being respectful. I knew how hard it was for you to confront it."

His face was too close to hers. "I've confronted it."

"No, you haven't. You can't stand it that the town knows. You can't stand it that anyone knows. Including me."

"It's *personal*."

"You aren't over it yet."

"Yes, I am. I went through years of therapy. I'm *fine*."

Wes studied her face. "Usually when a woman says *fine* like that it means the opposite."

She was starting to get really mad.

He held up his hand. "All I'm saying is you tell yourself you're fine when you aren't."

"That's because his *release* bothers me, and why shouldn't it? It would bother anybody. But I'm over being raped. I'm past that. He doesn't hold that over me anymore."

"Then why do you have to keep it a secret?"

That stopped her. He already knew why. It was her Jezebel past. She understood his point even though she didn't want to. He was right.

"It isn't your fault," he said in a deep, gentle voice that strummed her feelings for him.

But he'd betrayed her. "Why did you let me go on when I told you about it? Why didn't you stop me? Why didn't you tell me you already knew?"

"Lily…" He ran his fingers through his wonderful hair and sighed. "I'm sorry. I wanted you to tell me when you were ready."

He'd already told her that. "I trusted you."

"You still can. Nothing's changed."

"Talk about keeping secrets. How many others are you keeping from me?" She sprang to her feet and looked down at him, deep hurt engulfing her.

Wes stood, too.

She turned and would have left the office had he not taken hold of her arm just above the elbow and stopped her.

"Please. Let's not end the day like this," he said.

"I'm going back to your house to pack and get May and my dad."

"Lily…" But he released her arm.

"I'm going home, Wes." She turned again and once again tried to make it to the door, not caring that she left the cooler behind.

Wes took hold of her arm again, a little firmer this time, pulling her around to face him.

"I can't let you do that," he said.

Tugging her arm free, she stepped back and sent him what she hoped was a mean look. "What are you going to do? Force me to stay with you?"

"I don't want you alone right now."

"I have my dad and May."

"Two people who depend on *you*, not the other way around."

So many things were bouncing around in her head she couldn't keep up. How he'd pursued her. How careful he'd been with her. Because he'd known. And he hadn't told her.

He hadn't forgotten her past, either, the one that painted her reputation red. It's the reason he'd felt compelled to seek out the victims' officer. Instead of asking her, he'd gone behind her back. Because he didn't trust what she'd tell him.

"I know what you're thinking," he said. "I never questioned your integrity. That's not why I went to the victims' officer."

"No?" Her eyes began to sting with moisture.

His grew imploring. "Okay, maybe that was part of it. But you lied, Lily. I didn't think you'd tell me the truth if I asked you."

He was right, she probably wouldn't have. The realization

of that only upset her more. Maybe she wasn't over what happened to her. If she was, she wouldn't care so much that her secret had gotten out.

Fifteen years.

After all this time, she still wasn't over it. She'd done a great job of convincing herself that she was, but the truth wasn't going to change—no matter how much she wanted it to, no matter how much she tried to be strong. Her efforts were merely a smoke screen.

Wes moved closer, and in her distraction, she didn't think to escape him as he slipped his arms around her and pulled her close. "You're not the same woman you were when you left this town."

A tear slipped down her cheek. "That's not what you thought when you checked up on me behind my back."

He held her face between his hands, using his thumbs to wipe her tears—silent, unwanted tears.

"No. I knew you had changed. I knew that the day I met you, after I started talking to you."

She shook her head within the embrace of his hands. He couldn't have. He would have questioned her personally. Instead, he hadn't trusted her, Honey Creek's wayward wild child.

"We met at a prison, Lily." He sounded pleading. "I had to be sure."

She refused to let him break her resolve. His actions told her more than his words ever could.

"Then you should have told me after you were sure," she said quietly.

Pain and regret shadowed his eyes. This time when she slipped free of his arms he didn't stop her as she turned and headed for the door. But he followed her all the way to the Jeep.

When she opened the driver's door, he moved to stand

beside her. "Wait for me at home. At least do that much. I'm right behind you."

She didn't agree, nor did she disagree. She didn't know what she'd do. If she went back home, he'd no doubt have constant surveillance on her. Maybe he himself would provide the service. Continuing to stay with him would be hard, though. Knowing how he'd betrayed her trust, something that was already so fragile.

"Don't stop anywhere on the way home and keep your doors locked," he said. "After I pack up our things, I'll meet you there."

She looked straight ahead through the windshield.

"Lily?"

He wouldn't move unless she assured him. Finally she looked at him. She didn't want to assure him and she didn't want the sight of him to melt her.

"If I have to come after you, I will," he said.

And she knew he meant it. "It's just a little vandalism. No one is out to hurt me."

"I'd be inclined to believe that if the acts stopped with your truck. But someone tried to set the library on fire with you in it. That's a lot more serious."

Yes, it was serious, but she wasn't fooled. He was concerned out of more than his responsibility as sheriff. He had feelings for her. And that churned up conflict in her.

"Wait for me," he said again.

She met his eyes and didn't answer. It would be hard to pack her things and drag her daughter and her dad back to their house at this hour.

It wasn't until he shut her door that she realized the way he'd spoken. *Home. Our things.*

She looked at him through the driver's window. He stood with his arms at his sides, his face an expression of hard determination. She was the center of all that emotion.

Love and hurt waged a battle in her chest. More tears filled her eyes. She wiped them when they slipped free and put the Jeep into gear.

After throwing all the picnic paraphernalia back into the cooler, mentally kicking himself the entire time, Wes drove home faster than an off-duty sheriff should and finally pulled his SUV to a stop in front of his house. Leaving the cooler in the garage, he went inside.

It was surprisingly quiet. The Jeep was still in the driveway so he knew Lily hadn't left yet. He went upstairs to his room, hoping beyond hope that she'd had a change of heart and was there waiting for him. She wasn't. He went to her room door, wanting to knock.

"She's in there."

He turned to see May standing there.

"She was crying when she came home. She didn't see me."

Wes sighed hard and heavy and rubbed his tired eyes with his fingers.

"What happened?" she asked.

He lowered his hand. "Nothing. I just made a mistake, that's all."

The girl didn't look placated. Wes wondered if she was worried about Lily or something else.

"How much longer you grounded for?" he asked.

"Another week." She rubbed the toes of her right foot over the carpet, fidgety.

He looked from there to her face. Slowly May looked up at him. "Is she upset because…because of what everyone is…"

Dawning came over him. "It isn't your fault the rumors started in town, May."

Just as he'd thought, that was the crux of the girl's troubles. Her face sagged and her lower lip quivered.

"It was bound to get out sooner or later," he added.

"Yeah, but if I'd have kept my trap shut at that party..."

"You mean the party you should have never gone to?"

Her face reddened, probably more because he was a figure of authority rather than embarrassment over being caught at a party.

"I'm sure you didn't mean to hurt your mom."

"No."

"She's already over it." That wasn't true, but May didn't need to be bothered with that.

"Is she still mad at me?" May asked.

"She isn't mad at you for that. She's mad at you for lying and going out without telling her." And until he found whoever started that fire in the library, he wanted to make sure she didn't do it again.

"You still seeing that boy?" Lily had told him all about it.

"I see him at school."

"Are you going to go out with him again?"

She rubbed her toes over the carpet again, as though drawing an invisible line there. "I don't know."

"What will you do if he asks you to another party?"

"Tell my mom."

Good girl. "What will you do if she says no?"

She grunted and angled her head with growing annoyance. "It's stupid for her not to let me go out like all the other kids."

"It's not stupid. People haven't accepted her coming back here yet. She's concerned for your safety."

"Levi wouldn't let anything happen to me."

"What will you do if your mom says you can't go out with him?" he asked again.

She grunted cynically. "I won't go."

"Good, because if you don't listen to your mom, it'll be me coming to get you."

With that, May pivoted and started for the stairs.

"May?"

She stopped at the top of the stairs.

"I mean it."

The annoyance trying to make its way onto her face eased and she conceded with a nod before going downstairs.

Wes hoped to hell she'd do as her mom asked from now on. Otherwise, he was going to have his hands full.

Late the next day, Wes took the background checks on Amy Fordham and Eileen Curtis from Ryan and went into his office to start reading. He'd asked for a detailed search. Copies of everything. Birth certificates, Social Security numbers, marriage certificates. All of it. And it didn't take long to discover Eileen had some serious discrepancies in her past.

Eileen Curtis had grown up in a mountain town in southern California and had married in her early twenties. Wes found the marriage certificate which confirmed her married name— Williams. He looked through the file for a divorce decree and found none. Nowhere in the file could he find any indication that Eileen had divorced and taken back her maiden name.

If Eileen was really Tina, she was about the right age. Whoever had devised the ghost identity had known what they were doing except for the issue with Eileen's maiden name. Had Mark Walsh been that man or had he solicited the help of someone else? Wes would bet the latter.

He checked the file on Amy Fordham and confirmed what he thought he'd find; everything was in order. She'd had a rough go of things so far in her life, but she was an honest citizen with no criminal record.

It took him an hour to study the documents. When he'd

absorbed all he could, he dropped his pen down onto the stack and leaned back for a stretch. It was hard concentrating when his mind kept drifting to Lily.

He hoped he hadn't blown it with her. This morning he'd called home to make sure she hadn't packed and fled. When he discovered she hadn't, an overwhelming urge to see her hadn't left him alone. After he'd ordered her a dozen lilies delivered to the library, he'd had to force himself to stay focused on work. But now he was finished and all he wanted to do was see her. He also wanted to know if the note he'd sent along with the flowers had made any impact.

He checked the time on his computer. Five-forty. Her dad had said she was working until six tonight.

Grabbing his keys, he left.

When he entered the library ten minutes later, he searched for her. She wasn't in her office and he didn't see Emily. In fact, the library was nearly empty tonight.

He found her in the nonfiction section with a rolling cart of books she was putting back on shelves. She saw him as she turned to lift another one, going still, her eyes widening.

"Lily." He went to stand closer to her, the cart between them.

"What are you doing here?" she asked, resuming her task.

"I was going to see if you wanted to go get a bite to eat."

"Dad and May are cooking tonight."

Stiffness radiated from her. She was turning her back on him, but it took some effort. He almost smiled at that. Maybe the flowers had done some good.

"I'm sure they'll manage without us," he said.

She slid her eyes his way for a glance.

"Let's go out for dinner."

She put another book onto the shelf. "By the way, thanks for the flowers."

Okay, so she wasn't ready to agree to dinner. But she hadn't shot him down yet. "Don't mention it."

"I appreciate you apologizing, too." She rolled the cart farther down the aisle, seeming indifferent, or pretending to.

He followed, leaning a shoulder against the shelving, watching her beautiful profile. "Does that mean you won't move out?"

She looked at him. "I haven't moved in."

Not yet. Not technically. But now wasn't the time to tell her that's what he wanted. She'd only shoot him down, the way she was so good at doing.

"I would never do anything to intentionally hurt you. You know that, don't you?" he said.

After sliding a book onto the shelf, she bent her head.

"I didn't mean to hurt you, Lily."

"Well, you did."

"I'm sorry. I meant what I said on the card." He'd written that he'd done what he thought was right, what he thought she needed, but he was wrong and he was sorry. Would she please forgive him?

Her hands hadn't moved off the shelf after putting the book there. Slowly her head lifted and she met his eyes.

Touching her face with his hand, he caressed her soft skin with his thumb. "Please. Give me another chance."

Her eyes closed for a long blink. Then she opened them. "You're such a man."

"Thanks," he teased, but he knew what she really meant. Men could sure be stupid sometimes. When it came to women, sometimes they just didn't get it.

His cell phone started ringing. Bad timing. He didn't want to answer, but when he saw it was Ryan, he knew he had to.

"Sheriff."

It was Ryan and he could tell something was wrong. "Yeah. What have you got?"

"Just got a call from Kelley's Cookhouse. Damien's causing trouble with Amy Fordham."

"What kind of trouble?"

"Apparently he got in her face about a woman named Tina Mueller. Her boyfriend is with her and it doesn't look good."

"I'm on my way." He disconnected and looked at Lily. "Will you come with me?"

Her brow lifted. "To break up a fight?"

"No, I'll break up the fight. You wait for me and then we'll have dinner."

"There?"

She needed to face the world someday. The more time he spent with her the more it convinced him that's what would cure her once and for all of her past. She'd taught May to hold her head high, but she wasn't following her own advice. Avoiding places where the gossipmongers frequented was a sure sign of that.

"It's as good a place as any," he said.

She searched his face. "In case you haven't noticed, I'm working."

"It's six."

A tiny smile inched up on her face. "Let me guess—my dad told you that's when I got off."

He grinned. "He did."

"I wonder whose side he's on."

"Mine for sure."

She laughed softly. "Then how can I resist? When the men gang up on the women…"

"The women gang up on the men. Come on, let's get going before Damien tears the place down."

Leaving the cart, she walked toward the front. Emily was behind the counter.

"Call if you have any trouble closing," Lily said as she passed.

Wes followed her to his SUV. His heart burgeoned with gratification at her easy agreement in going along with him. He was making headway with her.

Getting there ahead of her to open the passenger door, he let her in first and went to the other side. Then he drove fast to Kelley's.

After parking in front of the restaurant, he got out and headed for the door, Lily right behind him.

Kelley's sounded more like a bar when they entered. People were shouting and talking loud and fast. Wes spotted Damien in a brawl with someone. Amy Fordham stood nearby, tears streaking her cheeks. Another Colton brother, Finn, was there, too, trying to talk to Damien. The two must have come here together while Finn was in town for a visit. An E.R. doctor in Bozeman, Finn was too brainy and congenial to do anything as Neanderthal as getting involved in a physical fight. He dressed impeccably and spoke well. His thick, light brown hair was a mess on top of his head, but he still managed to look groomed.

"Wait here," Wes said to Lily.

Watching the scene unfolding before her, she nodded.

Nudging people aside to get through the throng, Wes reached Damien and pulled him off a man.

"You're as crazy as your sister!" the man yelled at Damien, blood smearing on one side of his mouth.

Damien tried to yank free of Wes's grip, but Wes held firm. "What happened here?"

"Nothing. I heard her tell her boyfriend that you questioned her about Mark Walsh. All I wanted to do was ask her some questions."

"I don't know anything about Mark Walsh!" Amy yelled, and the man he'd fought with moved toward her, taking her into his arms. She cried against his chest while the man glared at Damien.

"What the hell, Damien?" Wes demanded, letting go of his arm.

"I didn't come here to fight. I asked Amy if I could talk to her and her boyfriend got between us. He said I couldn't talk to her, and I asked her if that's how she felt. Before she could answer for herself, her boyfriend shoved me and told me I should go back to prison. I shoved him back and he punched me."

"So you hit him back."

"Yes. He hit me because he knew who I was, not because of what I said to Amy."

Wes let that slide. "I already cleared Amy, Damien."

"Yeah, well, you didn't tell me."

"I was going to. You didn't give me a chance."

Damien looked over at Amy, who eyed him warily, a look that was becoming common whenever he appeared in public. The town didn't know what to think of him, and when he cornered people like this it didn't help. No doubt Amy would say he'd harassed her, the ex-convict who was supposed to be innocent now.

"It didn't get ugly until her boyfriend interfered," Finn pointed out.

"He got in her face!" the boyfriend snapped. "Amy told me all about him after you interrogated her."

Wes held up his hand, not liking the man's temper. The boy was new in town and obviously hadn't taken any time to question the gossip. Then he looked at Damien.

"That's true," Damien said. "Nothing would have happened if he hadn't lost his cool."

Wes looked over at the boyfriend. "That's bull crap," the man snapped.

"I was sitting at the table right next to them," said an older man, standing just behind Amy and her boyfriend. He pointed at Damien. "That man walked over to her and told her who he was and then asked her if she minded if he asked her a couple of questions. Her boyfriend got up and told him to get lost."

The boyfriend glared at the older man. Amy's sniffles began to ease.

Damien turned to Wes. "I just wanted to know what was going on."

Why hadn't he waited to talk to him? Did he doubt his abilities as sheriff? "You could have waited and asked me."

Damien's face eased into resignation.

Wes turned to Amy and her boyfriend. "I'm sorry about all of this. You can go now."

Amy looked indignantly from him to Damien, and then her boyfriend led her to their table, where they gathered their things and headed for the door.

Wes faced the crowd. "That's it, folks. Time to break it up." The people who'd gathered dispersed. Wes spotted Donald Kelley returning to his position behind the bar.

"Everyone's going to love that *he's as crazy as his sister* part," Finn said, earning a warning look from Damien.

Wes faced Damien. "I'll call you tomorrow. Good to see you, Finn."

Finn angled his head in acknowledgment, ever the gentleman, but clearly amused by the evening's happenings.

Wes turned and headed toward Lily. She smiled softly as he approached and the sight of it melted him all the way to his core.

He located the hostess. "Could you get us a booth?"

The slim blond woman nodded hesitantly. "Right this way."

At a booth, Lily slid onto the seat and he sat beside her. Damien appeared across from them, making room for Finn. Wes sent him a questioning look.

"You still have some explaining to do," Damien said. "And I don't want to wait until tomorrow."

"Mind if we join you?" Finn asked with a touch of sarcasm. He looked at Lily.

"I don't mind," she said, looking up at Wes.

Wes checked on Donald Kelley standing behind the bar, who nodded his consent. Apparently, the fight hadn't gotten too violent, or Donald would have wanted Damien to leave.

"Lily—Damien and Finn. Damien and Finn—Lily," Wes introduced them.

"Good to meet you, Lily. I've heard a lot about you," Finn said.

Wes inwardly grimaced at the innuendo.

Lily looked warily from him to Damien, who slouched against the seat, lazy and content. If Finn's comment bothered her, she did a grand job of hiding it. Instead of responding, though, she removed her silverware from the rolled napkin.

Damien eyed her before looking at Wes. "You never mentioned you had a girlfriend."

"It never came up."

Wes checked around the restaurant. Some people still glanced their way and talked, but others had resumed their evening. At least Damien hadn't busted anything.

"What do you do, Lily?" Finn asked.

"She took over for Mary Walsh over at the library," Wes answered for her.

"Lily Masterson. Yeah, now I remember you," Damien said.

Lily fingered her fork and lowered her gaze.

"Don't worry, I know what it's like to have the whole town talking about you."

"You have such a way with words, Damien," Finn said.

And Damien scowled at him. "And you don't?"

Finn looked perplexed.

A waitress arrived at their table, looking at Damien as she handed each of them a menu and put down four glasses of water.

Damien caught it and turned his scowl on her.

"I hope she doesn't spit in our food," Finn said.

He ignored his brother and turned to Wes. "Why don't you think Amy is the one who killed Walsh?"

"Her background checks out. There are no suspicious gaps and her maiden name checks out." He contemplated how to say what was next. "But Eileen Curtis's background gave me some different results."

"Eileen?"

"The real estate agent?" Finn asked, straightening in his seat. "Are you sure?"

Wes agreed Eileen was the most unlikely suspect. Her reputation was pure and everyone liked and respected her. She also fit the bill for someone motivated to ghost her identity. If she was, in truth, Tina Mueller, she had a criminal record from her youth that she wanted to escape. She wanted to assume another person's identity and live a normal life. But if she'd recently killed Mark Walsh, she hadn't deviated from her criminal ways and that made her dangerous.

"No, I'm not sure. Not yet." He looked pointedly at Damien. "I'm going to question Eileen again. Once I've done that, I'll call you."

"Thank you." Damien turned away and went a little still.

Wes followed that gaze and saw Lucy Walsh enter with three other people.

"Perfect," Damien muttered.

Lucy smiled as she talked to the man beside her. He was tall and lean with medium brown hair, and was dressed in jeans like her. Craig Warner and Jolene Walsh followed behind them. They were seated across the restaurant, but in plain view. Lucy happened to look their way and her smile drained when she saw Damien.

"I thought you didn't care about her anymore," Finn commented.

"I don't." But he sounded contemptuous.

The waitress returned to their table. "You folks ready to order?"

They did, with Damien still watching Lucy.

Lily turned to Wes, a question in her eyes. He wondered the same. How did Damien really feel about Lucy? He put his hand over hers and gave it a gentle squeeze, wishing they were alone and he could just stare at her.

Finn looked from their hands to Lily and then Wes. Wes ignored him and turned his attention to the table that had Damien so riveted.

Lucy leaned close to the man beside her. Steve Brown. Wes was pretty sure that was his name. Craig caught Wes's gaze and gave him a nod of acknowledgment. Wes tipped his water glass before taking a sip.

Steve said something to Lucy, caressing the top of her hand on the table and taking her hand in his.

Jolene's turn came. She noticed that everyone else at her table was looking somewhere so she did, too. And then her mouth opened and her eyes grew rounder. She seemed scared out of her skin. Wes didn't like the way the Walsh family had shunned the Coltons after Mark Walsh's debauched murder trial, but he also understood its source, and he knew with time that would all pass. Damien was innocent. They had all thought Damien killed Mark, but now things were different. Jolene had helped Wes by turning over the tape, and though he was inclined to believe she'd done it to protect herself, she'd also done the right thing.

A few minutes later he noticed Lucy say something to Steve, who glanced toward Damien and then said something in return. What had them so skittish? Or was it something else? Maybe Lucy didn't know how to handle Damien's return now that she knew he was innocent.

"Is he worried you're going to take her away from him?" Finn asked.

"I wouldn't take her back if she was the last woman in Montana."

"I wonder what she thinks of you now?"

"She probably feels bad for thinking you killed her father," Lily said.

Damien glanced over at Lucy, catching her staring at him. "She's probably afraid of me. She was so quick to accept the verdict, and she knew I was angry, and now, all these years later, come to find out she was wrong. Everyone was wrong."

Their food arrived and Wes dug in. Beside him, Lily did the same.

"What if Lucy does feel bad?" Finn asked. "Maybe she wants to talk to you, but doesn't know how to approach you?"

Damien turned his irritation on his brother. "That would be her problem. I forgave her a long time ago. And I've moved on."

"Yeah, it sounds that way to me," Finn quipped.

Wes knew that Damien felt betrayed by the town in which everyone had so easily believed his guilt, and Lucy's betrayal had been perhaps the hardest for him to take. Seeing her for the first time in fifteen years had to be a blow, whether he was over her or not. It had to dredge up old emotions and memories he likely didn't want cluttering his head.

No wonder he was irritated. Wes would be irritated, too.

"You both were so young back then," Lily said. "People

change over fifteen years. And no one can call you a guilty man anymore."

"Maybe she's afraid you'll ruin her newfound happiness," Finn said. "She might think you still have feelings for her. Or maybe she still has some for you."

"I don't think so. If she cared at all for me back then, she would have believed me."

Finn shrugged, chewing and swallowing before he spoke. "Well, all I'm saying is seeing you might bring a lot of memories back."

"I was in prison for fifteen years, Finn. I know that's easy for you to forget, but it isn't for me."

"I wasn't implying—"

"She's probably afraid I'll break into her house and strangle her," Damien said without waiting for Finn to finish, popping a French fry into his mouth.

That's how he thought the whole town perceived him, Wes thought. He couldn't stand that people couldn't accept his innocence. He was especially angry with their dad, who had barely done anything to help him. It was as if Darius had agreed with the jury like everyone else.

Darius Colton was a powerful man who liked to have his way and to have everyone in the family obey him. Some would call him selfish. Egotistical, even. But Darius Colton was also smart and relentlessly driven. Maybe success had made him callous. Wes didn't know. He was their father, that's all, whether or not any of them liked it. He had his redeeming qualities, but mostly he was just plain hard to please. Damien going to prison had only exacerbated that quality.

Lily leaned toward him and her scent reached him. Instantly, his attention floated to much more pleasant ground.

"For once the talk won't be about me," she said.

Meeting her eyes as she smiled at him, he thought he could look at her for hours and not get tired of the sight. She returned to her salad, almost finished with her meal, like him. The anticipation of going home with her permeated his senses. God, he loved her.

And it hit him.

He *was* in love with her. How did he feel about that? His mind reeled. Should he be more careful? What if she couldn't overcome her skeletons enough to accept him? To open her heart fully to him? What a cruel twist of fate that would be. For the first time ever, he'd found a woman he truly felt could go the distance and she might not feel the same.

But he wasn't going to give up. She was coming around. Her forgiveness over his going to the victims' officer proved it. She had feelings for him, she just hadn't let them loose yet. And he had some ideas on how to prod her along. Some intimate ideas.

"Let's go home," he said, his passion coming out in his tone.

She met his eyes and he caught a flash of response. Locked with him in silent communication, heat brewing between them, she nodded. A surge of satisfaction coursed through him. He hoped she didn't tear his heart out when this was all said and done.

Chapter 11

A tortuously sweet anxiety kept Lily's pulse heavy as she led Wes up the stairs. The house was quiet. At the top of the stairs, she walked slowly toward her room, wondering if she should stop and drag him with her. She was still upset that he'd gone behind her back with the victims' officer, but that didn't matter in the grand scheme of things. She could see that now. He hadn't meant to hurt her. He was only being what he'd always been. Careful with her and her well-being. That's what made her keep falling in love with him. How could she stay mad?

He took her hand when she started for her bedroom door. With a tug, she landed against him and met the intensity of his eyes. There was no mistaking his intent and the only answer in her heart was "yes."

She slid her arms around his shoulders, smiling her love. He kissed her and their passion erupted. He backed her into his bedroom and fell with her onto the bed.

She pulled his shirt up and he unbuttoned hers. He unclasped her bra and she threw it over the side of the bed. He got up to get out of his jeans and watched her shimmy out of hers while still on the bed. He pulled her underwear off and lay on top of her, holding himself up with his hands on the mattress. Both of them breathed heavy.

He didn't wait and she didn't want him to. He pushed into her with one smooth motion. Sensation burst into a ball of flame that spread from there. She couldn't get enough air, couldn't kiss him enough. She moaned.

He pulled back and slid inside, going slowly and not pulling back again until he was as deep as he could get. He did that several more times, torturing her with a maelstrom of sensation.

"Wes," she breathed. She felt hot and sweaty and shivery. The sensations made her tremble.

He groaned and began to move faster, impaling her with hard thrusts now. Her body jerked with each delicious pounding. Reaching above her head, she braced herself against the headboard, giving his thrusts more force.

She cried out her pleasure. He kissed her, taking the sounds into his mouth.

"Lily," he breathed her name as she had his.

"Oh, God." She was swept away on a tide of mind-numbing ecstasy.

Abandoning the headboard, she reached around him and grabbed his butt. She moved with him as he ground his hips against hers with each wet slide. He looked down at her, at her breasts as they jostled with his loving, and then lower. When he looked back up at her, he lowered his mouth to hers and kissed her. She ran her fingers into his hair, and then let her hands fall to the mattress, closing her eyes.

"Look at me," he whispered.

She opened her eyes and met the heat of his while he

pushed into her and withdrew. Another sound burst from her as a powerful release followed, endlessly pulsing. He groaned, going deep one last time and holding himself there as his orgasm joined hers.

"Lily." He kissed her cheek, her mouth. "I want you forever."

I want you forever, too. The words were in her throat, nearly making it to her tongue, but she stopped herself. This was the most gritty sex she'd had in more than fifteen years. She felt a little vulnerable, a little uncertain.

Wes lay on her, catching his breath along with her. It was an erotic feeling, lying beneath him with her knees still parted. Naked. Exposed.

Lifting his head, breathing more calmly now, he pressed a tender kiss to her mouth and then looked down at her.

"Are you okay?" he asked.

She nodded.

"I know. It was like that for me, too."

Powerful. Frightening.

"It's okay, Lily."

Was it?

He kissed her again and rolled to her side, pulling her back against him. They spooned. The sweetness of it warmed her. This was like nothing she'd experienced before. The urgency had some resemblance, but in all her wild encounters, none had held such poignancy. Relaxing in his arms, she let herself fall onto a cloud of love.

May waited for her mom to pick her up in front of the school, standing beside Levi. He made her feel so good. And everyone was starting to notice how much he liked her.

Yesterday, a girl on the cheerleading team had said hi to her. Today, she hadn't noticed any mean looks. How great it would be to have people start liking her!

"You think your mom will let me take you to dinner this Friday?" Levi asked.

"I don't know." She was grounded until then. "I can ask her." Maybe in her distraction she'd say yes.

"Text me when you find out."

"Okay."

He leaned toward her and her heart went like a rabbit when she felt him kiss her. Right in front of everybody!

But this morning her mom was acting different. And she was pretty sure it was because of Wes. They'd gone out to dinner or something and May heard them go into Wes's room together.

She swallowed all the heat swelling inside her and looked up into Levi's fantastic eyes. He smiled down at her.

"Wanna text all night?" he asked.

"Sure." She laughed and hoped it didn't sound too much like a girlish giggle.

She loved texting him. He was witty and cool.

"It sucks that you're grounded. I can't wait to take you out," Levi said. "I don't want to wait 'til Friday."

"Me neither."

"I gotta go. I'm supposed to drop some groceries off at my grandma's. But I'll text you as soon as I'm home, 'kay?"

"'Kay." She beamed.

He turned and walked away. She headed for the street, looking for her mom in Wes's Jeep. She wasn't here yet. A man standing outside a car caught her attention. Was he looking at her?

She couldn't see him from here. Was he a senior? His car was old and dented on the driver's door and the white paint was dull. She didn't know what kind of car it was. She stopped at the curb and waited for her mom.

The man didn't move. He was definitely looking at her. What for?

Spotting Wes's Jeep, she felt better. The guy gave her the creeps.

Getting into the Jeep, she shut the door.

"Hey, sweetie," her mom said. She looked really happy today.

"Hey. Did you and Wes make up?"

"What do you mean?"

"He said he made a mistake...and you're...I don't know... glowing."

Lily laughed briefly. "We aren't kids anymore, May."

"You did make up with him," May teased.

Her mom just kept smiling. May looked out the back window. The strange man had gotten into his car and now he had turned and driven the other way down the street. She'd see if he was there again tomorrow. If he was, she'd tell her mom. She faced forward and bolstered her nerve to ask her mom about Levi.

"Mom?"

"Yes?"

"Is it okay if I go out with Levi this Friday? He wants to take me to dinner."

Her mom looked at her dubiously.

"I promise that's all we'll do. I'm not lying this time. I swear."

"I'll think about it."

"I'm supposed to tell him tonight."

"Is he going to call you?"

"Text." All night! That just tickled her insides.

"Then tell him I have to think about it. He can wait a day."

May wanted to groan. She didn't want to wait. But she kept her mouth shut. Her mom might not let her go if she pushed too much.

* * *

The next day Lily still didn't know if she would let May go out with Levi. She handed a young woman her stack of books and saw Finn walk into the library. It was the middle of the afternoon. Was he here for a book or to see her? She was surprised when he came to stand at the counter.

"Hello, Lily."

"Finn?"

"I just wanted to stop by and tell you how glad I am that you and Wes are hitting it off."

Really?

"I didn't get a chance to tell you that the day before yesterday. When I said I'd heard a lot about you, I didn't mean…"

"It's okay. I'm used to it. It's nice of you to stop by and—"

"No. What I meant is that Wes has told me nothing but good things about you."

Oh. She perked up. "Really?"

"Yes. I mean, I've heard all the rumors like everyone else." He rolled his eyes. "How can you avoid it?" Then he smiled like a doctor who'd had a lot of face-to-face time with his patients. "But what he's told me about you just goes to show what a waste of energy all that is."

Lily felt her smile grow big. "Thank you."

"Don't mention it. I hope you and Wes make it as a couple. He's been alone too long. I'd like to see him happy."

A woman appeared behind Finn, checking out a rack of audio books located near the front counter. Finn saw her and went still. Lily wondered if he knew the woman.

She disappeared around the end of the rack and walked away, heading to another part of the library.

Finn turned away and faced Lily again.

"Someone you know?"

"Someone I haven't seen in years. Rachel Grant's cousin Carly."

"Oh, yeah. Bonnie Gene introduced me to Rachel once. How do you know her?"

"We went to school together." He got a faraway look, one tinged with what Lily could only call bitterness. "I'm glad she didn't see me."

"Don't want it getting back to Rachel that you're here, huh?" she teased. Clearly Rachel was a high-school love that he hadn't forgotten.

"I'd rather not have to deal with the drama."

Lily laughed lightly. "One of those, huh?"

He smiled, but it was full of derision. "I'll get out of your hair now. I just wanted to stop by and make sure you didn't misinterpret what I said."

"It's no trouble. Thanks for stopping by. I really appreciate it." Was it just her or were more and more people in town beginning to warm up to her?

Finn left and a few minutes later Wes came strolling in.

Lily shook her head, more from delight than amazement. "You just can't stay away from libraries, can you?"

"Only this one."

"It's a little early for dinner," she teased.

"I thought I'd make dinner for you tonight."

"It would be nice to see my daughter."

"Your dad, too."

That dimmed her spirit some. "He'd be happier having dinner with his nurse."

Wes chuckled. "Actually, I came here for a work-related reason."

There went the rest of her spirit. "Oh."

"But I'm not above using it for an excuse to see you."

She smiled.

"Someone came forward today about the flowers," he

said, growing serious. "A boy who lives in Karen Hathaway's neighborhood. He said she offered to pay him to buy the flowers and have them delivered to you."

What kind of person would put a kid up to that sort of thing? A disturbed one, that's for sure. The boy had probably carried his burden around, especially if he'd learned of the vandalized truck and the fire. "Did you confront Karen about it yet?"

He nodded. "And she confessed to the vandalism when I pressed her. She said finding out that you'd moved back upset her. It caused her to fight with her husband, even though when I questioned him he took her side. Just like the first time I talked to him."

"Jealousy can be so ugly."

"She denied trying to set the library on fire, though."

Lily stared at him as the implications of that sank in. "Do you believe her?"

"Yes. Sending flowers with a cryptic message and vandalizing someone's property are benign compared to trying to hurt someone."

Or worse. "Do you think whoever started the fire intended for me to die?"

"It had to cross their mind as a possibility. Yes, I think whoever started it was hoping you'd be trapped inside. Otherwise, why the library? They could have started your house on fire, but they singled you out. Your daughter and your dad would have been in the house. You were alone in the library. Somebody is mad as hell at you."

And Lily could think of only one person who had reason to be mad at her.

"Is there anyone else in town who might have the motive to hurt you?"

Lily shook her head. But then again…

"There are a lot of people who don't like me," she said.

"Yeah, but enough to start a building on fire?"

Lily turned, rubbing her arms. She felt sick to her stomach. "The victims' officer said Brandon moved to North Carolina."

"Yes, and I checked. He did move there."

She faced him again. What was going on?

"We don't have much to go on. The arsonist used a rock wrapped with rayon cloth, probably from a blouse. There's nowhere around here that sells that kind of thing, so the arsonist probably already had it with them when they came to throw it through the window."

Which could support the idea that Brandon had come from North Carolina, rayon cloth in tow.

"If it was Gates, I doubt he would have brought anything from his house or the house of any his relatives. Too much of a risk. If it was him, he probably bought the material, like a shirt, and picked up the rock on the way."

"It was him, wasn't it?" Lily felt numb inside. Was he going to try to hurt her again?

Wes sighed. "We don't know. I have someone checking to see if he left town. And let's not discount the possibility that it's someone in Honey Creek. Karen could be lying, too."

Maybe. But Lily wasn't comforted. She was going to start watching her back.

"What will happen to her?" Lily asked.

"She'll probably be fined and be forced to pay restitution and maybe serve some community service. She'll have to pay for your truck repair."

She nodded. Fair enough.

"I've got to go talk to Eileen Curtis now. What time do you get off?"

"I have to go pick up May from school."

"I'll meet you at home then."

Home. There was that word again. "Okay." She was warm and tingly everywhere.

He stepped closer, leaning in to kiss her. He moved his mouth over hers in a subtle but sexy caress, enflaming her in an instant. When he lifted his head, she was breathless and hot all over.

"Don't go anywhere else. Pick May up and go home, okay?"

She nodded, wanting him to kiss her again.

"I won't be long," he said.

He turned and left and Lily put her fingers over her lips, more in love than ever.

Wes walked into Curtis Real Estate and waited in the entry for Eileen to get off the phone. Several minutes later, she did and appeared in the doorway of her office.

"Sheriff." She sounded surprised. "Come in."

He went into her office and sat in a chair before her desk. She sat behind it, watching him warily. There was a vase of yellow roses on the desk and everything was tidy. Pictures on the wall were Mediterranean. Elegant. Didn't fit the profile of a killer.

But he had a job to do.

"I know your name isn't really Eileen Curtis," he said, knowing it would feel like a bomb dropping on her refined new world.

Her back stiffened, straightening her posture while her lips parted slightly. He saw her chest rise and fall faster.

"What do you mean?"

"You're real name is Tina Mueller. You left Atlanta after your stepfather was killed."

"That isn't my name."

He didn't argue with her. "I'm here to ask you where you were the night Mark Walsh was murdered."

"Wh-what…I don't understand. You think I killed him? Is that why you came here the last time?"

Last time he'd asked her about the first time Walsh had supposedly died. He hadn't asked her where she was when he was actually killed because he didn't want her to think she was a suspect. But the time was right now.

"I'm here to ask you some questions."

"I didn't kill anyone."

"You're wanted for murder in Atlanta."

"I am not."

"Eileen Curtis isn't, but Tina Mueller is."

"I told you, that isn't my name."

"Then you shouldn't have any problem answering my questions."

She didn't say anything and he wondered if she was contemplating whether to get a lawyer.

"Did Mark Walsh arrange for you to take over the identity of Eileen Curtis?"

Wes had spoken with her ex-husband over the phone and he'd never suspected a thing. She'd protected her identity very well. It only convinced Wes all the more how much she valued her freedom and her new way of life. But if she killed Walsh…

Still, she remained silent.

"Did he?" he pressed.

"I told you, I never met him."

"If your name is Tina Mueller, you did. I have a recording to prove it."

Her eyes were bright with clever processing. "I didn't kill anyone."

"Where were you on June 29 between seven and midnight?"

"I don't know. That was a long time ago. Are you accusing me of murder?"

"Not if you have an alibi." But then there was the issue of her stepfather's murder. The detective working the case wanted her extradited.

"I'll have to do some digging on that. Check my daytimer, and some receipts. My daytimer is in my purse. I'll go and get it."

She stood and went to another door off her office. She disappeared from view and Wes waited. When she didn't reappear, he felt a hunch and went after her. She wasn't in the adjoining room and the back door was open. Squealing tires and a roaring engine told him all he needed to know. He looked through the door and saw her white Lexus racing down the alley.

He ran to the front and jumped into his SUV, flipping on his siren and lights. Spotting her Lexus swinging onto Main Street, he wove around slower traffic to try and catch her. She turned a corner. He also turned there and saw her turn another one down the street. When he reached that he had lost her, but one of the turnoffs led to the highway. He headed there.

He saw her on the highway.

Racing after her, he closed the distance. She made it to Highway 90 and headed west.

Wes stayed on her bumper.

After five minutes, she must have realized she wasn't going to get away. She slowed and pulled off to the side. He drew his gun and approached her carefully.

She rolled her window down. Her cheeks were wet from tears.

"I didn't kill anyone," she said in a pathetic tone.

"Good. Let's fix it then. Will you get out of the car?"

She sniffled and opened the car door. Getting out, she didn't fight him as he handcuffed her and took her to the backseat of his SUV. He went back for her purse and then got behind the wheel.

"I'll have your car towed," he said.

But Eileen…or Tina just stared out the window.

He drove her to the sheriff's office and parked.

"Mark did give me all the papers I needed to start a new life," she said from the backseat. "In exchange, he made me… do things."

Wes didn't open his door to get out. Instead, he turned to look back at her. "What did he make you do?"

"He made me sleep with your father, Darius Colton."

Darius? Walsh had forced her to sleep with Wes's father? "Why?"

"He wanted me to try to find some bank account statements."

"Did you?"

"Yes, but they were nothing unusual. As far as I could tell it was a waste of time."

"Why did Mark want to see Darius's bank statements?"

"He never said, but knowing Mark, he wanted to find something to hold over Darius's head. Mark liked controlling people." Her shoulders quivered with a shudder. "He liked to control me, too, especially after I broke up with him."

"And he caught you stealing his wife's ring."

She wiped a tear that was rolling down her cheek. "Yes. Sometimes I wonder if he did it just to punish me."

"By making you sleep with Darius?"

"Darius is an… Sorry, I know he's your father, but he's not a very nice man, and Mark was angry that I broke up with him. It hurt his ego, so he needed to make me pay."

Wes didn't comment. Darius could be overbearing sometimes. But this whole idea of Walsh choosing Darius for Eileen to sleep with was peculiar. He must have had a reason to want to see the bank statements, but they'd shown nothing unusual. Had Walsh wondered if Darius was involved in money-laundering? That didn't make any sense. Darius had more money than he knew what to do with. Why would he want to get his hands dirty when he didn't even need to?

More likely Walsh wanted to find a way to control Darius, just as Eileen said. And to punish her.

"How many statements did you give Walsh?" he asked.

"A whole year's worth. And there was more than one account. I'm pretty sure it was everything Darius had. I slept with him twice. Once to get the statements and once to put them back after I made copies." Her shoulders shuddered again. "It was awful. He's a terrible lover. A selfish one."

Wes ignored her retrospection. This was his father they were talking about. "Did you keep any copies for yourself?"

"No. Are you kidding? Back then, all I wanted was for Mark to leave me alone. I was glad when I heard he'd been killed."

"Did he ever contact you?"

"No."

"Not ever? Not even when he came back to Honey Creek?"

"No. I never heard from him. And if I had, I don't know what I would have done."

"Would you have killed him?"

"I told you, I didn't kill anyone." She looked right at him in the rearview mirror and Wes had a creeping feeling that she was telling the truth.

"Who killed your stepfather, then?"

Her expression closed and she looked out the window.

Was she hiding something? He'd be sure to let Detective Isaac know what he thought.

Chapter 12

Lily parked in front of the school and watched all the kids climb into buses, walk, ride bikes or get into their parents' cars. When the crowds began to thin, she started to wonder where her daughter was.

The buses drove away and soon there were only one or two stragglers milling around. Lily got out of the Jeep and went inside the school. Finding the office, she asked the secretary to page her daughter. When that didn't produce May, Lily asked where her last class was. She went there, but it was dark and empty.

Her heart beat fast. She was getting scared. May. Where was she?

She called Wes's house. No one answered.

She called May's cell phone. Nothing. Wes's cell came next. No answer.

Her dad didn't have a cell phone.

Driving toward Wes's house, she tried to calm her trembling hands. What if something had happened to May?

Her cell rang, making her body jerk. She looked at the number. It was May.

"Oh, thank God." Relief washed through her as she pressed the button to connect the call. "May. Where are you?"

"Mom?" May sounded shaky. And she was crying.

Dread plunged to her core. "May? Where are you? Are you all right?"

"Lily, Lily, Lily," said a man's voice. He must have taken the phone away from May.

Oh God, oh God, oh God.

"I've been waiting a long time for this."

Brandon.

"If you so much as touch my daughter, I'll tear your eyes out with my bare fingers."

"Just outside town is an unmarked road. It's past an old cabin that's falling apart. You'll see it on the right."

She knew the one he meant.

"I want you to take that road until it forks. Take the left route until it dead ends. You'll see my camper."

"You let her go or I'll make sure you die before anyone can send you back to prison."

"You come here, sweet Lily, and you come alone, or the girl will take your place. If you call anyone for help, I'll kill her. Understand?"

Lily couldn't find her voice.

Brandon disconnected.

Swallowing, she breathed through her nausea. To think of him doing to May what he'd done to her…

She'd kill him.

Lily swung the Jeep around and floored it on the highway. She wasn't far from the cabin.

Should she call the cops? 911? No. He'd kill May if he heard sirens.

Wes.

She brought his number up in her cell phone address book and pressed Send. It rang and rang and he didn't pick up. Where was he? What was he doing?

His message system beeped. "Wes, this is Lily. Brandon has May. He's kidnapped her." She did her best to describe the area where he'd taken her. "He warned me to come alone. He said he'd kill May if I didn't do as he said. He said he'd kill her, Wes." She knew she sounded frantic, but she *was* frantic.

She came to the dirt road and flew down it. She had to reach May. She didn't want to leave her alone with that monster. But she didn't have a gun. Or a knife.

A pen would work. If she could stab one of his eyeballs maybe it would penetrate to his brain. She leaned over to the glove box and dug around. The Jeep swerved with her effort. She found a pen.

A camper came into view. She slid the Jeep to a halt and waited, leaving it running. She wanted him to come outside, hoping he'd have May with him.

The door opened and he stood there, curling his index finger, beckoning her to come to him. Damn it.

Tucking her cell in her back pocket, she got out of the Jeep, holding the pen at her side. Slowly she approached, seeing a gun tucked into the front of his jeans.

"Where is she?" Lily stopped walking. "Show her to me."

Brandon jerked his head at where May must be, and she stumbled next to him.

"Mom!" May shoved Brandon and raced for her. Lily caught her daughter against her and guided her so she stood behind her.

"Did he hurt you, baby?" she asked, watching Brandon step down the stairs of the camper. He looked a little unsteady. Had he been drinking?

"No." May was crying.

Lily reached behind her and took May's hand, pressing it against her back pocket.

Sniffling and beginning to regain control, May slipped the phone from the pocket as Brandon drew near.

"Run," Lily said. "Get to the Jeep." It was still running.

"I don't want to leave you."

"Do what I tell you. Run. Now."

Brandon pulled the gun from his jeans and aimed for the Jeep. He fired and one of the front tires blew.

Lily's heart crushed under the weight of apprehension. Now what?

Pushing off Lily's back, May started running. She went for the Jeep anyway.

"May!" Lily shouted. Then, to her horror, she saw Brandon aiming his gun at May.

She charged for him. He wasn't far from her now. The gun went off. She tackled him, landing on top of him on the ground. Her right leg felt funny and it took her a second or two to realize she'd been shot.

He punched her and then hit her with the gun. She got dizzy and disoriented and fell off him. The pen slipped from her fingers and fell to the ground. Brandon started to climb to his feet.

Determined, she pushed him the same time she swung her leg back over him, straddling him and stopping him from standing. He moved the aim of the gun toward her. She grabbed it with both hands and deflected his aim as he fired again. She picked up the pen and stabbed him, going for his eye but hitting his cheek.

He yelled and smacked her hand away. Lily stood and

kicked his wrist, the one that held the gun. It flew from his grasp.

Staggering, her leg not supporting her well, she kicked the gun so that it skittered across the gravel surface, out of his reach.

He sprang to his feet and bashed her head with his fist again. This time it knocked her to the ground and her vision fogged. She was vaguely aware of him going toward the Jeep.

"Run, May!" she yelled. "Get out of here!"

She was getting weak. Rolling to her butt, she saw blood soaking her jeans. She was bleeding. Badly.

May was fighting Brandon off, kicking at him from the driver's seat and struggling to keep him from taking the cell phone from her. She dropped the phone and Brandon picked it up. She tried to take it from him. When he smacked her, Lily saw red.

She rolled to her hands and knees and crawled toward the gun. Hearing May cry out, she looked back. Brandon was dragging her from the Jeep. But May bit his hand and he yelped. She got away.

"Run, May!" Lily screamed.

And she did. May bolted down the road.

Lily reached the gun and took hold of it. Rolling onto her backside, she started firing.

Leaving Eileen in the holding cell, Wes went back to his SUV for his phone. He checked the screen and saw Lily had tried him twice. A sense of extreme foreboding slammed him. And then he heard someone shouting.

"Sheriff! Sheriff!"

He looked up to see a boy running toward him. Levi Harrison, the boy May was seeing.

"You gotta come quick!" He waved his cell in front of him,

skidding to a stop in front of him. "It's May. Somebody's got her and her mom. She called me, but she got disconnected when he caught her. She tried to tell me where they were, but he cut her off."

"Get in."

In the SUV, Wes dialed his voice mail. Lily's voice streamed fast, telling him what he needed to know. He raced for the west end of town, lights and siren blaring for the second time today.

Damn it. He'd have gotten her call before now if he'd had his phone with him, but the drama with Eileen had preoccupied him.

The campsite wasn't far outside of town. He swerved onto the dirt road and saw May jogging wearily along the side. Wes stopped and Levi jumped out to help her. She was crying hysterically. Levi held her and guided her into the SUV, seating her in the middle and holding her to his side.

May babbled incoherently about what had happened. Brandon shooting out the tire, fighting her until she got away.

Shooting Lily….

Wes could hardly contain his fear. Or his fury. Minutes later he reached the dead end. He saw the Jeep and two bodies. His fear escalated until his head felt bloodless.

He faced the two teenagers. "You two stay here. Don't move."

Levi nodded.

May leaned forward, her hand on the dash, searching the scene in front of them. "Is my mom all right?"

"Stay here," Wes repeated. He handed the radio to Levi. "Tell Ryan to send an ambulance."

Levi took the radio and when Wes saw that he knew how to use it, he shut the driver's door and ran toward the bodies. One was Brandon Gates, shot in the chest and neck. He wasn't moving and looked dead. There was no gun on the ground next to him so he passed him and went to Lily.

She lay sprawled on the ground a little farther away, a gun close to her unmoving hand.

"Lily." He knelt beside her and checked for breathing. It was warm and glorious against his cheek. He felt for a pulse. Weak, but there.

He looked back to see a thumbs-up from Levi.

Help was on the way.

Chapter 13

Lily woke to bright lights and stabbing pain in her right thigh. Lifting the covers over her, she saw a bandage. It all came rushing back. She searched the room. Wes sat in a chair beside her, his head bowed in sleep. There were flowers everywhere. Who were they from?

She rolled her head to see Wes again. Watching him sleep took her mind off the pain.

As if sensing her stirring, his eyes opened and his head straightened, his gaze finding hers. In the next instant, he came alert and propelled himself from the chair to go to her, leaning over her, sliding one hand alongside her head and taking her hand with the other.

She smiled.

He kissed her. "I'm so glad you're awake."

"What happened?"

"You were shot in the right thigh and it nicked your femoral artery. You lost a lot of blood. The doctor was confident, but wouldn't say with any certainty that you were going to make it." He kissed her again. "We were so worried."

"We?"

"Your dad and May were here. They went home this morning to rest, but they'll be back soon. You had surgery last night. It was late when they finished."

"Lily."

She looked toward the door where the voice had come from. Her dad stood there, his face a contortion of relief and repentance. He walked into the room.

Wes stood, giving her hand a squeeze. "I'll give you two a few minutes."

And she realized he and Shay must have talked.

Wes left the room and her dad moved the chair closer to the bed and sat. He clasped his hands between his knees and took a moment before he began. Finally he looked up at her.

"Lily...I'm sorry. When Wes called and told me what happened, I thought of losing you before..." He got a little choked up.

"It's okay," she said, reaching her hand out.

He took it between both of his. "I don't want to leave this earth without knowing my daughter. Because I don't really know you, Lily."

Moisture burned her eyes. She'd wanted this for so long. Her dad.

"I can see you've changed," he continued. "And I also realize your mom and I could have done things differently with you when you were growing up. I should have been there for you more."

"I'm not looking back. I made a lot of mistakes. You aren't to blame for those decisions."

"You *are* different now, Lily. And it breaks my heart to know what happened to you is the reason you changed."

"I like to think I would have changed anyway." She smiled.

"Then that's the way I'll think of it, too." He looked toward the flowers on the windowsill and on the counter across the room. Color exploded everywhere.

"Between Wes and Levi, the whole town knows you're here," he said. "Mary and Jake Pierson sent flowers. So did Bonnie Gene and her husband. Finn, too."

Recalling what Finn had told her about Rachel, Lily wondered how long before the two ran into each other. It would be quite a spectacle. More gossip for the town, that's for sure. Something new to focus on.

"Maisie Colton even sent you something," Shay said. "It's the big bouquet of yellow roses."

"Maisie sent flowers?"

"Wes told her what happened. He also told her he was going to marry you so she'd better change her tune where you're concerned. So she sent flowers." Shay laughed wryly.

The words gave her a jolt. Marry her?

"Won't be long before the whole town sees what I do now," he said. "A strong woman who's full of integrity."

"Dad." She wiped the tear that slid down her cheek.

"You've done a great job with May. I can't wait to spend the rest of my days with the two of you. It'll take some time, but I want us to be a family."

"Oh, Dad." She cried and he got up to lean in for a hug. She couldn't ask for anything better.

A few days after coming home to Wes's house from the hospital, Lily was beginning to wonder if she was overstaying her welcome. Wes had brought her here, but now that Karen had been caught and Brandon was dead, there was really no reason for her to stay any longer.

Wes hadn't mentioned anything about what her dad told

her. Not that she was worried. She felt more like pinching herself. Having a man like him love her seemed surreal. Too good to be true. But why hadn't he said anything? Did he not want to marry her after all? Had he only said that to her father because of the drama surrounding her injury?

She hobbled downstairs after taking a late-afternoon nap. A news program played on the television. Stormy weather was on the way.

Wes was at the kitchen table, poring over his notes. He looked up and smiled.

"I was going to come up and wake you if you didn't come down soon," he said.

"Really?" She looked around the house. It was too quiet. "Where are Dad and May?"

"They went out for a while."

"Out?"

"Yeah. Grandpa-and-granddaughter time."

That made her smile. "Where did they go?"

"They didn't say."

"Huh." She supposed that wasn't odd. Maybe it was the way Wes told her, as if he were trying to be nonchalant.

He pushed his chair back and stood. "You hungry? How about we go out for dinner?"

"You want to go out?"

"Yeah. Let's go down to Kelley's. You feel up to it?"

"Uh…sure." Actually, she felt great. She was moving around without crutches now. She limped, but at least she was getting better. But he was acting funny.

"What's the matter?" she asked.

"Nothing. I just feel like going out. We've been cooped up in this house for days."

He'd gone to work, though.

"Okay." She looked down at herself. Baggy jeans and a

long-sleeved, ribbed, white T-shirt. All she needed were shoes and those were by the door.

She put them on and eyed Wes as she made her way out the door. He was smothering a grin.

"What are you up to?"

"Nothing. I'm hungry." He wiggled his eyebrows. "For more than food."

They hadn't made love since she'd been shot. It would hurt too much, according to him anyway. But maybe not now. After dinner, if…

Wes opened the passenger door of his SUV and helped her inside. His cell rang as he climbed onto the driver's seat. He answered and his mood sobered.

"Detective Isaac," he said, glancing at Lily. He seemed surprised.

She waited while he listened.

"Then Tina was telling the truth," he said after a few moments, and then more minutes passed while he listened again.

"Thanks for letting me know." Shortly thereafter, he ended the call.

"What happened?" Lily asked.

"That was the detective who worked the Tina Mueller case in Atlanta," he explained. "He said a woman came forward and confessed to killing Tina's stepfather. She was fifteen when he kidnapped her and kept her in the basement." Wes looked over at her, his face revealing what the detective must have told him about what Tina's stepfather had done to the girl. Kept her for a sex slave in his basement. "Tina managed to leave a butcher knife in the basement for the girl, and the next time the stepfather came down for one of his visits, the girl killed him. Just before that, that same night, he beat up Tina, who saw the girl kill him and helped her cover it up. They were afraid of being charged with murder."

"What happened to the girl?" Lily asked.

"She went back home and told her parents that she ran away. She didn't tell anyone about Tina's stepfather."

"What will happen to them now?"

"I don't know. They can probably prove self-defense. Tina gave the girl a knife so she could defend herself."

Lily wondered if Tina would come back to Honey Creek. Would the town support that? After what Lily had endured, she didn't hold much hope for the woman.

Wes parked down the street from Kelley's. There were a lot of cars out tonight.

"Everybody must have decided to go out for dinner tonight," she said, and then she eyed him and wondered again. What was he up to?

He opened the door for her and she entered. Kelley's was packed.

Bonnie Gene appeared, smiling from ear to ear. "It's good to see you up and about, Lily. Come here. We have a table ready for you."

Bonnie Gene led her to a table in the middle of the restaurant. Lily sat, but Wes remained standing. Only then did Lily notice the occupants of the tables surrounding her.

Finn. Damien. Mary and Jake. Maisie and her entourage of friends. Maisie smiled and waved but it appeared forced. She wasn't enjoying herself. Lily smiled back anyway. Then she saw May and her dad. May giggled and Lily slid her gaze up to Wes.

"Grandpa-and-granddaughter time?" she queried.

He grinned and reached into the front pocket of his jeans. "Lily Masterson," he said, loud enough for everyone in the now-quiet restaurant to hear. "There's no other woman for me."

He held out a ring. The elongated garnet center stone was flanked by two round diamonds. Simple but elegant.

She looked from it to Wes.

"Will you marry me?" he asked.

She sprang to her feet, putting most of her weight on her good leg, and wrapped her arms around him. Planting kisses on his mouth and all over his face, she could only laugh her joy.

"It took you long enough," she teased.

"Is that a yes?" he said between kisses to his mouth.

"Yes!"

Everyone in the restaurant cheered. It was a homecoming. At last she was accepted. There was nothing in her closet to hide, and nothing to run from. She was home.

* * * * *

COMING NEXT MONTH

Available September 28, 2010

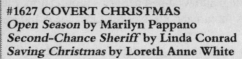

ROMANTIC SUSPENSE

SRSCNM0910